THE FOOLS OF GOD

BY THE SAME AUTHOR

The Harlequin Edition

THE FOOLS OF GOD

Julian Fane

Book Guild Publishing
Sussex, England

First published in Great Britain in 2008 by
The Book Guild Ltd
Pavilion View
19 New Road
Brighton, BN1 1UF

Typesetting in Garamond by
Keyboard Services, Luton, Bedfordshire

Printed in Great Britain by
CPI Antony Rowe

A catalogue record for this book is available from
The British Library

ISBN 978 1 84624 195 6

CONTENTS

THE BAND OF HOPE

Magdalen, called Magda
Winifred, called Winnie
Noah
Phillis, called Phil
Rudolph, called Rudy
Adeline, called Addie
Zachariah, called Zac
Vivian, called Viv

PARENTS

Once upon a time, in the last century, nearly a century ago, to be imprecise, it all began to happen.

A father and a mother of eight children were called Lord and Lady Penzoote of Penzoote in the county of Cornwall. Their Christian names were Edward and Mary. The old family name, dating back to long before the creation of the barony, was Hope – the children were little Hopes.

The Penzootes took their privileges in their stride. They rose above their status. They did not live luxuriously. They were neither straight nor inverted snobs. They were as good as classless as it is possible for a Lord and a Lady to be.

The barony of Penzoote rewarded a Joseph Hope who had tried to guide Disraeli through the maze of his debts. Joseph was a Mr Fixit of his day. His son, Noah, the second Baron, was notable only in so far as he sired Edward, third Baron, and eventually the father of the eight Hope children. He was now thirty-eight years of age. He had been an only child. He had lost both his parents in a freak accident at sea. He therefore inherited the title in 1907, and in the year after that he courted his future wife.

Penzoote is a village on the southern coast of Cornwall. Joseph Hope chose that name for his barony because he had bought and largely rebuilt a fake Georgian castle on a promontory about half a mile from Penzoote village. The house was Castle Scar, which had pretty fortifications and a round tower and arrow slits. It was located on the top of a rocky outcrop, a scar, the base of which was washed at high tides by the rolling breakers of the Atlantic Ocean.

Castle Scar was a landmark at sea and on land, especially at night when its windows glowed with golden light. During storms, the family always turned on the lights in the attic of the tower to warn sailors not to founder on the rocks below. The castle had a good-sized garden with gardener's cottage. Beyond was a lane leading through farmland to the village and the coastal highway.

On a summer's evening in 1907 Edward Penzoote descended the zigzag path to the beach below Castle Scar. Farmer Hanslip, his neighbour, had been out fishing with a couple of his farmhands; they were now selling their catch of mackerel to the village people – there was a different public path to the beach winding round and down the scar. He and Edward greeted each other with a wave, and a moment or two later Jack Hanslip came across to talk to him. Jack was the older man, sixtyish, red-cheeked, and his family and the Hopes had been friends for many years. The Hanslips belonged to a class no longer recognised or known, they were yeomen, practical and prosperous, tillers of the land and sometimes landowners, higher up the social ladder than farm workers and not so high as gentlemen farmers. Jack was the owner of Seascape Farm's three hundred acres that encircled the Penzootes' property.

When they met Jack touched his cap with a respectful gesture, but called Edward by his Christian name: no wonder foreigners can never understand the English social system!

'Sorry about your people, Edward,' he said. 'I couldn't get to the memorial service and I've wanted the chance to give you condolences.'

Edward expressed gratitude. They exchanged views of the cruelty of the sea.

Jack remarked: 'Well, you're the lord now.'

'With more responsibilities,' Edward commented ruefully.

'Will you carry on at the Castle?'

'It should be full of children.'

'That's a point. Any plans in that direction?'

'Maybe.'

'Local?'

'Maybe.'

'You always was a dark horse, Edward.'

'Can I ask you something?'

'Is it a favour?'

'Sort of.'

'Out with it!'

'You've a daughter, Jack.'

'I've two of them.'

'The younger one.'

'Are you going to blow me down?'

5

'Not yet. I'm getting on for forty – and I've put off the evil hour – and now I'm the last of my line. I need to do my bit. And I can't dawdle. Do you catch my meaning?'

'Make it easier for me to catch!'

'I'm healthy to the best of my knowledge, and fit, and I've a home and an income, and I'm a Catholic like you and keep my word. Would you object to me asking your Mary a question?'

'Well I never!'

'If it's cheek of me to ask, Jack, I'm sorry – but I know a good girl when I see one – and I've known Mary a long time.'

'You're offering us a step-up.'

'I'd only ask her. And I'll take no for an answer.'

'She's just out of this here finishing school for girls.'

'I'd do my best for her.'

'We'll see, shall us? I'll ask the first question.'

'Thank you very much.'

A day or two later Edward met Mary in the village by chance. He was entering the Post Office with a letter to be stamped, she was coming out with a small bag of sweets. She flushed scarlet, a promising sign for a would-be lover. He smiled at her while they stopped in their tracks, facing each other – she did not hide her head despite the blush.

'Hullo, Mary,' he said.

She laughed and offered him a pear drop. He took one and thanked her. She laughed again and scurried past him.

She was shy but not gawky. Her laughter was not silly or out of place. He had no second thoughts.

The next step was that Jack Hanslip called at Castle Scar. He and Edward conferred briefly at the front door.

'She'll see what you've got to say for yourself, the saucy minx,' Jack said.

'She suits me.'

'You should take the older one, Edward. Nothing wrong with Violet.'

'I'm sure that's true.'

'My missis says come to tea, then you can choose.'

'Yes, Jack, but I have chosen.'

'What about tea?'

'I'll come if I can see Mary alone.'

'Well, now it's up to you two.'

They shook hands.

On the appointed day Edward reported to Seascape Farm. Jack showed him into the sitting-room of the farmhouse, the parlour, which was full of red plush and smelt unused. Mary entered and closed the door behind her. She was again blushing and looked hot; but she was a brave bold girl, stood her ground, smiled at him and seemed to be repressing her high spirits and laughter.

He began: 'You only know me by sight,' and paused; 'but you know why I'm here.'

'Yes,' she said clearly.

'I'm not doing this right. I'm afraid I'm impatient, and I don't stick to the rules. Your father will have told you the pros and cons.' He took a deep breath and burst out: 'If you'd marry me one day, Mary, I'd love you truly.'

'You're far above me,' she said.

'I don't see it that way. I'm nearly twice your age. I have to be in London off and on. And I like a quiet life. Sorry – I can't help rushing you, but I wouldn't rush when we have an understanding, and could start to understand each other. If there's a war I'd have to do my bit, so I might not be worrying you for long.'

'All right.'

'What did you say?'

'All right.'

'Do you mean yes?'

'Yes.'

'I didn't mean to blackmail you. I wouldn't harm you ever deliberately.'

'You've made me proud.'

'And you, you make me humble and grateful.'

She laughed and he joined in.

'Tea's laid in the kitchen,' she said.

Her family had inside information: in the kitchen it was all kisses and congratulation. Edward's future wife was in the arms of her father; his future mother-in-law was explaining that she had wanted him to see that they were 'kitchen people'; his future sister-in-law hugged him as he had not yet hugged Mary; and her half-brother Tom, son of Jack's first and late wife, was crushing his hand; and the laughter was like wedding bells.

The period of the engagement of Edward and

Mary was as unconventional as the proposal. It was abbreviated at Mary's request. The Hanslips raised no objections to her spending time alone with her fiancé at Castle Scar. She soon proved she was an amorous tactile girl, although the religious faith they had in common prohibited pre-marital sex. Her excitement and exuberance was his delight, and she loved him for his learning and wisdom, and for so kindly loving her. They agreed not to go anywhere for the honeymoon, just to be stay-at-homes and be happy together.

The consequences were the birth of Magdalen in the first year of the marriage, the birth of Winifred in the second, and the births of Noah, Phillis, Rudolph, Adeline and Zachariah in successive years after that. The eighth child, Vivian, was born after the outbreak of war in 1914, and Edward's volunteering for active service in the army.

He had worked in the City of London before he inherited from his father – he was a City gent. He was in banking, and then a stockbroker. He had been a handsome young man with blond hair parted on the left hand side and brushed back flat, regular features, blue eyes, and stood six feet tall in his socks. He was competent and successful. He moved in a social set not exclusively of golden youths, he and his business friends were all trying hard to make a living. Edward attracted girls, but Edward thought they were not the right ones, and the girls seemed to think likewise. Why? He had a detached quality, he was not like the other boys, he was too serious

9

for frivolous fillies, he was a Roman Catholic and might not be easy to get away from. He was disappointed, but, on reflection and in time, not disheartened. None of the girls who had turned him down really fitted into his image of Castle Scar. He did not wish to serve a life sentence in the company of any of them. He preferred to wait and see.

Mary Penzoote née Hanslip, the younger of the two girls at Seascape Farm, who had worn pigtails and a plate, appeared before her husband in the transformed guise of Cinderella – not at a ball, and not that he thought of himself as a prince, but at their wedding, when she made her vows, and in their bedroom and their nursery.

Edward never said much about his war in the trenches, in hospitals, in transit between the two, and his awful leaves, so looked forward to, so bitter sweet, and almost at once filled with dread because he would have to return to active service, to mud and blood. When it was all over, he limped home to Mary and his children, Magda, Winnie, Noah, Phil, Rudy, Addie, Zac and Viv.

The war changed Edward and Mary along with everyone else involved. Edward was more sombre, Mary more grown-up, and they loved each other more deeply and were more religious. The Penzootes agreed to celebrate by making a structural alteration within Castle Scar. They removed the door between the sitting-room and the chapel that was part of the original design of the building. It was a discreet alteration – the entrance to the chapel was at the far end of the sitting-room. A further change inside the chapel was explanatory. On one of its white walls they installed a marble plaque measuring six inches by six inches on which was carved, 'Thank you E and M 1919'.

Change did not stop there. The old gardener at Castle Scar, Mr Timms, had followed his wife to the grave on the day the Armistice was signed. Edward offered the job and the cottage to Jones, who had served in his regiment and become his top non-commissioned officer. Private Jones was transferred into Second Lieutenant Hope's platoon in 1914. They had risen through the ranks together, and saved each other's life on numberless occasions. They were demobilised as Major Hope and Sergeant Jones.

Jack Jones, always known to the Hope family as Jones, had worked on his father's small-holding pre-war, he knew a bit about husbandry and was keen to learn gardening. He came to Castle Scar on a day trip. He not only loved it, he fell in love with the young housemaid, Jean Watson, daughter of a Penzoote family. They married, moved into the gardener's cottage, and Jean was soon pregnant.

Meanwhile Mary turned out to have a constitution that enabled her to look after her husband, their brood, their staff, Jones and Jean and Mrs Clark, their cook, most of the inhabitants of Penzoote, and still have the energy to enjoy it all, to laugh and be the cause of laughter.

The rustic maiden of yesteryear had developed into a fine-looking woman with a glowing complexion and an open jolly regard. Her shiny brown hair was held up by combs as a rule. Edward praised her 'well-turned' ankles. Her optimism seemed to fill her home with a pleasing scent. And her optimism was tempered by realism. Her frown was as influential as her smile. A critical word was the more effective for differing from her eagerness to praise. She ruled the roost of Castle Scar, but for and on behalf of her husband, who gave her confidence, and was keeping his vow to love her only and for ever.

Their honeymoon continued to be postponed – it was a joke between them. She said, and he admitted, that she was needed at home, and to travel anywhere with eight children in tow would not have much honey about it. Besides, Edward was a fixture at Castle Scar. He was unemployed – that is, he worked long hours at being a gentleman of leisure. He had books to read – reading was a closed book to Mary. He studied newspapers and corresponded with the stockbrokers who had been his colleagues before the war. He had to have time to himself, to think, prune his roses, discuss world affairs with Jones, and sit in the chapel – Mary and then the children recognised the limits of his capacity for sociability and yen for solitude.

He was apt to call himself eccentric. He was aware of not doing what he could have been expected to do. He steered clear of London and had never taken his seat in Parliament's House of Lords. He joined no political party, he went to no parties. He gave Mary a marriage settlement so that she had a personal account, put money in another household account in their joint names, and was as un-stingy as he could afford to be, although he dressed in old clothes and drove an old car, and his children wore hand-me-downs. He was approachable by all and sundry, but also had a private life, maritally, religiously, also financially. He had not lost his interest in the Stock Market, and was the cautious 'contrarian' type of investor. He made the money he was able to set aside for his children during the German inflation in the twenties and the later crash on Wall Street.

Both Edward and Mary woke early in their bedroom looking down on the ocean. They had breakfast before the children had theirs. With luck, he was able to retreat into his study for at least some of the morning, but she had chores to attend to, and usually they were both called upon to get children to school of one sort and another, or classes, or friends' houses, or doctors. In the course of the day there were bound to be outdoor or indoor games, swimming in the sea, bicycle rides, homework, quarrels to be made up, moods to be changed, injuries to be treated, and in the evenings the round of 'good nights' and 'sleep tights' in the bedrooms decorated with posters of film stars, sporting gear, girls' hats, boys' cricket 'colours' in the shape of caps.

Summer was Castle Scar's season. The family, sometimes including Edward, almost lived on the beach in the bay, in the sea or on it. They shared it with Mary's relations, with villagers, locals, and employees. After picnic teas the toddlers were led back to the Castle and the village by Mary and other parents carrying picnic baskets, rugs, buckets and spades. The older children, and more children as they grew up, were allowed to stay late to catch the tide for surfing, to dive off rocks into the deeper water or play rounders in the wide expanse of ridged sand at low tide. Magda and Winnie were allowed to be in charge of two or three of their juniors at dusk, even after night had fallen. If youths from the village joined in, there were challenges and banter about swimming in the nude; but the shrieks and the bellows, drifting up and through open French windows, sounded like guarantees of harmless fun, and the young people would obey the calls that it was bedtime from above.

In those summer months the interior of Castle Scar smelt of sand and plimsolls. The limbs of the little children were gilded with sand and the hairs beginning to grow on older legs were sprinkled with it, like letters in days of yore. Sand was always being washed out of the long hair of girls, and lips tasted of salt. Happy days, carefree days! Did it rain much? Occasionally there would be a thunderstorm, sheet-lightning flashed along the Cornish coastline and thunder threatened to split the sky, and then heavy drops of rain comparable to summer fruits splashed against window panes. Gales were inclined to keep the thunderstorms company, and the children of the castle would be mobilised by their father to help him and Jones to pull the rowing-boats farther up the beach and beyond the reach of the great angry waves. But such manifestations of the wrath of God were not heralds of the end of the world. Storms subsided, the sea was again as docile as a good dog. The sun in heaven smiled on Castle Scar.

In the evenings of days without clouds, when dew seemed to fall like manna from heaven on the earth, Edward Penzoote liked a stroll through his garden to enjoy the scents of flowers, released as if to thank for the goodness of the weather. And he would pass Garden Cottage, where Jones lived with Jean and their children, James and Iris. Jones justified the name of his dwelling by filling its plot of land with horticulture galore, a handkerchief of lawn, a rocky area, beds of seasonal colour, rows of vegetables, and a couple of apple trees. He too enjoyed a spell by himself in the gathering dusk, and the two men would chat over the picket fence. In the garden and elsewhere, attending to cars and mowing machines, they spent a lot of time together, but were never short of something to say.

On one particular evening in the 1930s, Edward and Jones were thus engaged in conversation. They had commented on the crying need for rain, as country folk do.

'What do you make of the news?' Edward asked.

'That's it,' Jones replied.

The exchange was not so meaningless as it might appear to be in black and white. Edward was comparing the weather with the international situation, and Jones was referring to the vagaries of luck.

'What do they want with a man like that?'

Jones was casting aspersions on Adolf Hitler, Chancellor of Germany, Leader of the Nazi Party.

'You may well ask.'

'Are we going to have to fight him next?'

'Goodness knows!'

After a pause Edward added: 'I've intended to talk to you about those shares we bought.'

He had given Jones some of the shares in German industry he had bought cheap a few years previously.

'They've done well,' Jones remarked.

'It might be an idea to sell them and take a profit.'

'Up to you, sir – we're grateful to you for thinking of us.'

Edward said: 'The Bolsheviks are to blame, they threaten everyone and frighten us all to death. Goodness knows where it'll end! Too many crooks are spoiling the broth.'

Jones's comment, 'Oh ah,' had multiple meanings – it expressed interest, agreement, enlightenment, sympathy, positive and negative reactions, and neutrality.

'I think we should move our money out of harm's way,' Edward said.

'Where would that be, sir?'

'America – but we're patriotic, we'll want the money in this country if or when the balloon goes up. We could keep it under our beds.'

'You give me papers that need signing, sir.'

'Okay – I'll try not to lose your money.'

'Thank you.'

'Should be fine tomorrow, shouldn't it?'

'Looks that way.'

'Better make the most of it.'

'Is news that bad?'

'No. You ought to know how pessimistic I am by now. Ask my wife – she'll tell you everything is just about perfect.'

'Oh well – she's not far wrong. Respects to the lady.'

'Good night, Jones.'

'And many of them, sir!'

CHILDREN

At first they were like warm puppies, tumbling about, squealing, bawling, fighting, going to sleep on top of one another. They were so close in years that they shared the same pram, the same cot, the same clothes. So far as anyone could see there were no bad ones – Mary thought them all good. Viv was the youngest. When he was born the oldest, Magda, was nearly ten.

Edward and Mary's eight children in their early years lived up to their surname, Hope, not only in the adult eyes of their mother. Their closeness touched the hearts of outsiders. Magda was sweet to her younger sister Winnie, and so it went on from one sibling to the next. Each child always had someone to play with. But they understood each other better than they were understood by the majority of grown-ups. They mutely begged to differ. They were different after all, their home was Castle Scar, where they could hide and lose themselves. And their walks were not bread-and-butter exercise, they were fraught with risk and danger – they lived by the sea which was always ready to snatch and drown a child, and they had to descend a precipitous path to get to the beach at the bottom of their garden. There was swimming, too, they were taught to swim for safety and then were dared by their siblings to duck through storm-tossed waves.

They were united and reunited by intelligence. Their contemporaries at school were not the children of a lord and lady, nor did they live in a big house with an alarming name, and nor were they so quick at book-work, at speaking and writing English, at memorising and sums. They were duller into the bargain, although the Hopes were not consciously intolerant or arrogant. Naturally Magda and the other seven preferred the company of siblings who shared their experience, saw their jokes, and with whom they could compete in testing games and debate and argue on equal terms.

The last of their bonds was not the least. They were baptised in the annexe of their sitting-room that was a Roman Catholic chapel by a priest of Rome called Father O'Malley. They were imbued with the faith of their parents. They were educated in that faith in their primary schools. Some of the Hope children continued their education in Catholic establishments, but one or two went to C of E schools that specialised in a particular subject of tuition: Addie and Viv, for instance, who had scientific interests. Sectarianism was introduced into childish minds, and Catholicism set the Hopes apart from their protestant Cornish social contacts and their protestant schoolfellows.

Moreover, they inherited a form of the social

disinclinations of their father. Edward's tendencies were accentuated at the time of his marriage – Mary sufficed for company thereafter, Mary was the world he wanted to live in. Then the war induced a sort of revulsion from the human race, from the mass of its representatives who could do and did such horrible things to one another.

The Hope children signalled their self-sufficiency. The younger ones sought shelter under the wings of their elders. Schools were hurried home from in order to be with brothers and sisters. Hopes had a way of staring at children bearing other names as if at men from Mars. They seemed to find it difficult to play with strangers – the village boys and girls were vaguely recognised by those who lived in the castle, but the salt sea was only a temporary sort of leveller. Recreation in winter for Hopes took an eccentric turn as minds developed along with bodies. There was a craze for speaking words backwards. Sometimes they communicated in pidgin versions of French and Russian – Magda and Noah were born linguists; sometimes they only used the manual language of the deaf and dumb. A favourite competition was to have to define the meaning of words on a page of the dictionary – the winner defined the most words correctly.

The idea that Castle Scar was a greenhouse forcing the growth of intellect occurred to Edward. He discussed it with Mary, who could see nothing wrong in her children being clever.

He tried it out on Jones.

'Can't stop them being what they are,' Jones said.

'They seem to be a bit too keen to amuse me.'

'Only right and proper – my children do that.'

'I foresee my lot turning into teachers called Chalky.'

'I wouldn't have no objection to mine getting white-collar jobs.'

'Oh well!'

'Not long past we weren't expecting to have children, were we, sir?'

'That's a good point.'

Edward, however, could not detach himself from a phase in his children's development. His rearrangement of access to the Castle's chapel was the measure of his attitude to God. He liked God better than people in general, and had wished to be able to spend time in God's room, so to speak, without hindrance. He often sat there, facing the table that served as an altar with its wooden cross and the stained glass in the window above catching the morning sun. Although he was more religious than his parents had been, he had assumed that his children would react to the Bible in his own way.

They took it too much to heart. The first three or four children, after having Genesis read aloud to them and hearing Father O'Malley's explanatory chat, refused to eat apples for months. A later child, Zachariah, pushed a drawing-pin into the palm of his left hand to see what it would have been like for Jesus to suffer the nails. At around the age of eleven several children developed religious mania. They spent too long in the chapel, they knelt too long praying at bedtime and were not pleased to be told to hurry up for pity's sake by their mother. Magda and Phil felt they were called to be nuns and lazy Rudy thought life in a monastery would suit him.

Common sense was a casualty of the religious epidemic. All eight children caught it more or less badly in their early years. They were not interested in, they refused to listen to, their father's urgings in the direction of moderation. They lectured their mother, who got into trouble for saying that she had no time for sanctimonious talk. They argued over interpretations of biblical advice, 'Love thy neighbour', for example, even to the point of fisticuffs and bleeding noses.

Relief arrived in the shape of a joke. Magda made it – at fourteen she was receiving contradictory calls from nature. She asked her father: 'In what part of the body is the soul?' Edward struggled to answer, but eventually he and Mary had to laugh. Then Magda laughed – it was never established whether or not she had meant to be funny. In ensuing days, weeks, even years, the other children revelled in the teasing and tickling naughtiness of Magda's seemingly innocent inquiry. One winter evening the lights went out in the sitting-room and a frightening figure in white could be seen dancing round in the firelight, terrifying the young ones, startling everybody, and moaning that it was the Holy Ghost.

Laughter reconstituted common sense. There were no more letters from schoolmasters worried by the belligerent proselytising of the Hope boys and girls, and no more complaints from parents whose children had been called names, 'atheists' and 'pagans'. Laughter again rang out in the rooms of Castle Scar, where puritanical silences had been holding sway. But Edward continued to have secret fears that his children might never shake off that taint of the idealism of their precocious religiosity.

The search for love was healthier than the craze for high seriousness. Magda at sixteen could and would have been a wife in many societies past and present. She and Winnie, aged fifteen, and even Phil heading for her teens, were reincarnations of the girls who had danced round the Maypole. They were the flowers opening to the spring of life, or the fruits ready for eating. Noah, too, was of age physically. He had spots and bristles, and a husky muscular frame. The love-bug affected the younger children, they all began to read cheap romances instead of the biographies of missionaries and martyrs.

Predictably, suitable members of the opposite sex did not grow on the trees shaped by gales that grew in the Castle Spar region of Cornwall. The Hopes had not been taken to children's parties. The Hopes had stared at the children who might by now be growing into Romeos and *femme fatales*. They had to make do and mend, or fall back on imagination and abstinence.

The era they were living in was not permissive.

They were too young, moral, cautious to take the risks productive of fates worse than death – they were not yet so unconventional as to go where Dame Nature beckoned. The summer swimming ceased to be so 'mixed' as it had been. The female Hopes ruled out late evening sport in the phosphorescent waves, and the male ones complained that the village maidens were more like sluts.

Magda, and in due course her siblings, had recourse to education in its wider sense. Edward had prophesised that his children were bound for the Groves of Academe. A combination of logic and sex starvation lured them to where contemporaries with similar interests and urges must lurk amongst the greenery.

Magda won scholarships. She was to read history for three years, and, she was sure, learn more basic lessons. She was doubly disappointed.

She clashed with her tutors immediately. She asserted that history was a matter of opinion. She said, wrote and believed that history was only authenticated for the individual by faith. Her tutors were down on her like a ton of bricks – she was discrediting their research and making mock of their teaching.

She fared no better in her sexual studies. Female students in the 1930s were a tiny minority, shielded and shackled by regulations, and expected not to draw attention to themselves by means of make-up, attire, immoral behaviour, or the advancement of radical ideas or provocative theories. The average lady graduate seldom raised her bespectacled eyes from her books, and her stockings were blue with a vengeance.

Magda rebelled. Her bad luck was that she was not so pretty as to be pursued and brought to bay by carnivorous male youth in the singular or plural. She was tall, large and had strong features as well as strong views. She took up with a fellow Catholic called Piers De'Athe. He was reading theology, was willowy, prudish, snobbish and proud of his unpronounceable name and long lineage. After two terms of holding hands she gave him a proper kiss, from which he emerged gasping as if he had been drowned. She dropped Piers after that, and he was obviously relieved, which was not good for her self-respect.

Winnie was much prettier than Magda, she had blonde curls and big blue eyes, yet was twice unlucky. She got involved with Trevor Connolly, a biologist, who was all too keen to mate with her, but he was an oversexed atheist, she could not trust him, was terrified of having a baby and the wrong baby, and fought him off for a year: after which he got another girl in the family way and was forced to marry her. Winnie's next 'flame' was Peter Purefoy, whose surname had three syllables. He was reading English and attempting to write it, a poet in theory, who dressed poetically and was soulful. She grew quite fond of Peter, although he was so self-centred and self-conscious. She invited him down to Castle Scar, but he did not fit in there, the other Hopes thought him hopeless, and he said adieu to Winnie at the end of his visit. He said that in the bosom of her family he had felt like Daniel in the lions' den.

Noah struck up a friendship with a Croatian girl at university, Franzine was her Christian name, and he too brought her down to Castle Scar; but she was another dud. She was much bigger and stronger than he was, and her idea of a caress was to lift him up and squeeze him until he begged for mercy.

All Edward and Mary's children left university with more or less brilliant degrees, but had formed no worthwhile or lasting attachments, failed worldly examinations, made no money, and were frustrated. They suffered from feeling that they had been unjustly treated. They came round to agreeing that they would have to find or create a world or worlds in which each of them would be recognised and rewarded.

Agreement was reached not in so many words or on paper, but by the allusive tick-tack of families.

They said: 'We can't go on like this... Our country's badly governed... We must help everybody... We need to climb greasy poles... For God's sake, of course!'

And the echoes came back: 'Far-reaching solutions, not short-term fixes... Laying foundations... For charity, for happiness... God will not be shut out, but we have to clean up the mess by secular methods.'

Their plans reached the ears of their parents, who were pleased to have their children at home, at Castle Scar, as in the old days. There was a general uplift of spirits after the somewhat gloomy years of university education. Mary was impressed by the pretensions of her offspring, and giggled to think of them aspiring to be so high and mighty. Edward listened and smiled benevolently.

Again he had recourse to conversation with Jones across the picket fence of Garden Cottage.

'They shouldn't be here, you know,' he told Jones, referring to his children who were children no more. 'They shouldn't hang around their mother and me, and Castle Scar.'

'They've got ideas for going places, sir – Miss Magda was telling me.'

'They think they'll be able to change our country, they're not the first English people to think that.'

'It's change in the future they're on about.'

'How are they going to do it?'

'They haven't told me, sir.'

'No, they wouldn't, they couldn't. If they're reinventing the future, I suppose we'll never know whether or not they've succeeded.'

'We could do with a better world, I'd say.'

'Yes, but … Change is usually for the worse.'

'You wouldn't want the old days, sir, would you? They was cruel to horses.'

'Thanks, Jones. No, I wouldn't. But I have my doubts and my fears.'

'Yes, sir.'

MAGDALEN

It was never established for certain who invented
the term descriptive of the eight children of the
Penzootes. It came into being in the early 1930s,
and was adopted by all of them enthusiastically.
The four words of that term were: The Band of
Hope.

Of course it referred to their surnames; but
they liked it more for the reference to their social
consciences and visions of the possible betterment
of the lives of the governed. They were apolitical
in principle, although their ideas might boil down
to politics in practice. They did not react
mechanically against the conservatism of their
parents, they themselves were traditionalists –
traditionalists with open minds, they said. They
could see the fatal flaw in socialism as well as
the charm of some of socialism's nostrums: for
socialism refused to take into account the
ambitions of *homo sapiens*, its competitive instincts,
and therefore socialist jaw-jaw about soaking the
rich and enriching the poor was always
contradicted by corruption, by socialists plotting
to be more equal than others. Again, they saw
the point of a Liberal political party, they were
liberals with a small l, but also saw that politically

it was disastrous to be the pig in the middle, and usually meant that Liberals weakened the opposition to bad laws and bad characters gaining ascendancy. As for Marxism and communism, they were foreign, revolutionary, dogmatic and surely suspect: that was the consensus, although Noah tended to disagree.

The Band of Hope paid lip service to the fashionable tenets of the idealistic classes. They were against war, if uneasily: what about their father's military background and his and Jones's war-wounds? They were against the death penalty, capital punishment: but still more uneasily – their father and Jones had killed Germans who were not even guilty of civil crime; and what was to be done with young men who kill, can they be kept in cages at great expense for ever? They thought almost everyone was hard done by: women, the poor, criminals, prisoners, divorcees, pensioners, the chronically sick, dunces, and so on. They reluctantly went along with criticism of the British Empire, and the idea that some African colonies were ready to govern themselves democratically and without too much bloodshed. But their eyes were fixed on a landscape beyond front gardens and the middle distance, they visualised the beautiful blue miasma of the future, illuminated by shafts of light from heaven.

Their unassuming aim was to leave the world a better place than they found it – modesty was not their strongest suit. Why should they be falsely modest, they had proved their cleverness, and they knew they had God on their side? They had settled the question of religion to their satisfaction. They had worked it all out at home, at university, and in their hearts. They were faithful, they were in favour of faith. Religion was faith in what was beyond proof, atheism was merely faith that faith in what was not proven was untenable. Religion helped you, atheism did not help: the choice was simple, they preferred the positive and helpful.

For Magda, the eldest of the eight, membership of the Band of Hope was a prop and substitute. She had passed her twenty-first birthday long ago. She was an accomplished young woman, tall, strongly built and apt to be clumsy. In fact and in truth, she was a galumphing girl. Her face had good features but was inexpressive, she was ready for love but lacked sex appeal – she had not attracted even one lover as yet. She had finished with university, was still living at Castle Scar, and restlessly rushing through books of every description, true romances, studies of phallic women through the ages, Gibbon's *Decline and Fall of the Roman Empire*, and the works of Sir Walter Scott. She never met a man, not counting her father, brothers and Jones. She was afraid that if it had not been for the Band of Hope she might have gone dotty. She was convinced that the Band would do great things, but worried that she herself had no particular plan in mind, and, more so, that none of them had any means to the ends they envisaged – they had written no best-selling tracts or monographs, were not politicians or preachers, were dreaming their dream in a vacuum.

This was approximately the background to Magda's decision of travel to Germany. She would go with Cornelia Hicksen, a German-born widow of a Penzoote man, William Hicksen, a dealer in antiques. Cornelia was known to the Hopes through Rudy who had gone to her for lessons in German, one of his many languages. She was now in her later fifties, and wanted to return to her native land to see relations and collect certain papers. She was a white-haired woman, cultured, extremely polite, and had renounced her German nationality – she was a British citizen with passport to match.

They arrived in Berlin and were taken under the wings of Cornelia's connections. They stayed there for eleven days, first with people called Veill, then with another couple called Grunning. These people were much older than Magda, but welcomed her warmly into their houses and conversed with her in a mixture of their English and her German. She did some sight-seeing, and was included in some of the luncheon and tea parties to which Cornelia was invited. For the last four days of their visit they went to Nuremberg.

Magda was typically intellectual in that she was short of common knowledge. She knew that Adolf Hitler was the new Chancellor of Germany, and that with his fiery oratory he was putting his country back on its feet and on the international map. She was interested in him and in how he was doing it, but was equipped with no answers to such questions. Gradually, in Cornelia's company and from their hosts and hostesses, she picked up information and messages often in code.

Cornelia was non-committal about the modern history of her native land. She said Magda would have to judge Hitler for herself – she would be able to read German newspapers and listen to Hitler and his ministers on the wireless. When Magda broached the subject of politics at social occasions, Herr Veill, Herr Grunning, and Herr Wels, her host in Nuremberg, and their Fraus, all looked at her as if she had dropped a brick. But they were grown-ups, the older generation, she did not bother her head with their concerns, their untranslated sharp exchanges, their arguing after she had gone to bed, for Germany had stirred her latent energies.

Her youth was reactivated. Suddenly she seemed to be surrounded by men, beautiful young men in glamorous uniforms. She felt her eyes growing rounder, she was aware of ogling, she accepted every compliment of a glance in her direction, a stare by a teutonic Apollo in field-grey, and returned it with a smile, a warm ocular welcome. The tensions in the air of Berlin had tonic effects on her soul, or, more accurately, her libido. She was on holiday from books and exams, and not averse to new experience.

It happened on the day after they – Magda and Cornelia – arrived in Nuremberg. Cornelia had an appointment with a lawyer called Herr Walter, Magda remained in the waiting-room. Cornelia rejoined her with Herr Walter in tow, who was an Anglophile and had wished to meet the English girl. Following the introduction and pleasantries, he wished to know what Magda was making of Germany. Her admiration was so glowing and sincere that he invited her to attend a Nazi Party rally on that very evening – he and his wife had taken tickets but he was not free to attend – Magda would sit in his seat and see the Chancellor of Germany addressing his troops.

She was picked up from the Wels' house at seven-thirty – it was the month of October and dark by that time. Frau Walter was a smart middle-aged lady wrapped in furs, and her car was chauffeur-driven. Their seats were in a grandstand overlooking a vast expanse of concrete – a parade ground, according to Frau Walter. At eight, the lights in the stands were switched off and brilliant lighting was switched on and directed at the towering flagpoles with red flags brandishing black swastikas on the edges of the parade ground. Applause broke out, people clapped the dramatic effect. Trumpeters were then caught in spotlights, their brass instruments glinted and shimmered, and the martial music blasted out. It stopped abruptly, unexpectedly, and soldiers in those spotless uniforms were marching across the concrete and forming into geometric patterns. More and more soldiers in strict regimental order were positioning themselves in straight lines, in blocks, in silence except for the tattoo of their booted feet. They were in squares, which were filling gradually, and now the bands struck up as flag-carriers, the flags showing regimental crests and heraldic designs, entered and marched through passages flanked by soldiery to their appointed places.

When all was ready for the main event, and the whole parade ground was packed with soldiers and flags furling and unfurling, the many thousands of spectators applauded for many minutes.

The lights going out put a stop to it. The parade ground was in darkness, only the flags on the tall flagpoles were visible against the dark night sky. This time the silence was prolonged.

'What's next?' Magda whispered breathlessly, because she was so excited, to Frau Walter.

'You'll see, my dear,' Frau Walter replied in her heavily accented English.

At last a spotlight shone on the wide central aisle between the massed troops. It was empty. But in the distance, at the far end, a small figure moved, was advancing towards the rostrum at the other end of the aisle. A great moan of applause, involuntary, purposeful, turned into rhythmic clapping, while the soldiers stood rigidly to attention and only their flags fluttered. The figure, Hitler, wore a brown uniform, not the soldiers' grey, with a military cap and a swastika armband, and walked, not marched, along the aisle. He was quite small and his black moustache was unimpressive to the point of being an absurdity. Yet Magda, watching him, unable to take her eyes off him, was on the receiving end of a sword-thrust of passion. It was more than love at first sight. It was unique for her and incomparable – the untapped resources of her body and soul were swept into and submerged in the aura of his achievement, popularity, success and power.

Frau Walter jogged her elbow and whispered: 'What do you think?'

Magda wanted to say, 'Amazing, marvellous,' but the words stuck in her throat, could not get past the lump in her throat, and by way of answer she had to glance at her hostess with tears welling into her eyes.

Frau Walter laughed under her breath and mouthed the word, 'Wait!'

Hitler had mounted steps to the rostrum. He was a short distance from where Magda sat. He was such a little man dominating such a large crowd – the pathos of him and the greatness tore at her heartstrings. Eventually the clapping tailed off, the only light shone on Hitler, who began to speak in short sentences, quietly and without notes. She could not understand a word of it; she could not concentrate on it, but her passion was not for words. His voice rose and rose again, he was yelling harshly and gesticulating. He stopped and again the huge moan and then the cheering erupted. Magda felt as if electric shocks were coursing up and down her spine.

The speech continued, quiet and loud, peaceful and belligerent, frightening, compelling, and was followed by the loudest and longest cheering, Hitler's retreat through a door at the back of the rostrum, the trumpets and the band playing marches, the dispersal of the troops with their flags, and the clearance of the grandstands.

Back in the car, Magda was teased for having

been bowled over by Hitler. Frau Walter told her she was a born Nazi and inquired in a jocular tone of voice: 'I believe you would not like to meet your hero, would you?'

'Oh but I would, I would,' Magda entreated.

Frau Walter laughed and said in her peculiar English: 'For that, I will be your fairy godmother, I will take you to a tea-reception tomorrow afternoon. Is it a pact?'

Magda's response was a tearful hug.

At the Wels' house she rang the doorbell and was admitted by Cornelia, who hurried her into the privacy of the dining-room and announced that she would have to cut her time in Germany short and would be returning to England early the next morning. She was apologetic, but said that Magda could stay with Hans and Maggi Wels for the remainder of her holiday – it was all fixed and the Wels family would be pleased to have her to themselves.

Magda, in spite of her unreceptive mood, grasped the gist of this announcement, at least the part that affected her, and belatedly noticed Cornelia's agitation.

She asked: 'Is something wrong?'

'No, nothing, don't worry, I don't want to spoil your visit. How did you get on this evening?'

Magda could not hold back, her emotions gushed out in a torrent of words, descriptions, declarations, confessions.

Cornelia sat down in a heap on one of the dining-room chairs and covered her eyes with her hands.

41

Magda was startled, and begged her to explain. Cornelia at last supplied answers.

'You cannot speak of Hitler in such a way, you cannot, Magdalen! You don't know what you have said. You don't know how little you know. You heard Hitler promising to persecute my race, and you love him – no! I am a Jew. I had to leave Germany for that reason. Again I have to leave Germany because I might be traced through the papers I have collected and could be in danger of imprisonment and worse. All my friends who have been kind to you, they are the people Hitler rages against and threatens to destroy. Please do not love Hitler!'

'I don't know what to say.'

'Say nothing. Now – would you like to come home with me instead of encouraging Hitler by staying in his country?'

'I can't – no, no – I don't want to leave tomorrow – I don't. Have you exaggerated? I can't believe Hitler's so wicked. I think he wants good things for the German people.'

'How could he? They're criminals.'

'Who are?'

'The Nazi Party, his party, and they stop at nothing.'

'I don't think that's true.'

'My dear, you are too young to say that to me.'

'I'm sorry, but...'

'Listen, listen, I shall leave this house at eight in the morning. If you wish to come with me, I'll see you here, downstairs, at eight. Good night, Magdalen.'

Magda's night was actually sleepless, and no doubt the same applied to Cornelia. She was confused, her young head spun, and the love of her heart seemed to be under attack from hateful facts and experience. She cursed her ignorance of current affairs. She could not rebut Cornelia's charges, she lacked the arguments. She wanted to contradict, but could not disregard some of Cornelia's information, for instance that she was Jewish, her friends were Jews, and that Hitler had publicised his baleful antagonism to their race. Yet racialism was another void, she had never encountered it in Cornwall, she had never been bullied for being Cornish, no one had ever been deliberately nasty to her for being what she was – were the innocent Jews really being imprisoned? And what was worse for them than imprisonment? Possibly the Nazi Party was cruel – it was military – soldiers were historically apt to be rough – that was their job, but Hitler did not walk like a soldier, he slouched. And his insignificance combined with his enormous strength were the characteristics that had sealed her fate.

Into this maelstrom of inner debate and hysteria strode the Band of Hope in Magda's imagination. For Hitler had the quality their Band required in order to reach its goals. She loved him in a roundabout way for being what her brothers and sisters could have done with, a powerful individual, a mover of mountains. He was the personification of the wherewithal her siblings were waiting and she herself had subconsciously pined for.

At eight the next day she heard Cornelia Hicksen leave the Wels' house. She was obstinate, she was guilty, and was not giving up Hitler for anybody or anything. Her future was apparently condensed into whatever could or would happen at the tea-reception, to which Frau Walter was taking her at four o'clock.

She ate an awkward and hurried breakfast with Herr and Frau Wels – nobody mentioned Hitler – and mooned about in the city of Nuremberg until three o'clock. At four Frau Walter arrived, and they were driven to a big house where the social gathering was already under way.

Too many people were present to allow proper introductions, a few hands were waved in the direction of Frau Walter, and they sat on a brocaded settee in a vast room and were offered cups of tea and rich little cakes on a cake-stand.

After a quarter of an hour the chatter was hushed, all those sitting down stood up, space was created near a doorway, and Hitler with his host and hostess entered the room.

Magda had understood that the party was meant to be informal – therefore no applause or social rituals. But it was certainly ritualistic by English standards. Hitler was seated in a line of gilt chairs, offered tea which he refused, and guests were brought forward to sit beside him, first one on his right for a snatch of conversation, then one on his left while another guest replaced the one on his right. Everybody stood except the Chancellor and the two replaceable conversationalists sitting briefly on either side of him. After about twenty minutes Hitler rose to his feet and began to walk round the room between lines of guests, acknowledging by a nod or a smile the kowtows of the gentlemen and the respectful bobs of the ladies.

As he approached Frau Walter, Magda whispered to her: 'Can I speak to him – alone – please!'

Frau Walter shook her head; but after she had curtseyed and shaken hands, she indicated Magda and murmured a sentence in an excusatory tone. Hitler smiled and extended his hand, which Magda clasped and kissed as she curtseyed almost to the floor. She did not let go of his hand, instead she drew him, tugged him almost, a few steps into an alcove behind where they had been standing. She was boiling hot, as if with a high temperature, curtseyed again and stammered while tears ran down her cheeks: '*Mein Fuhrer . . . Mein Fuhrer . . .* I am in love with you.'

He raised his eyebrows, inclined his head, and said: 'Thank you, *danke*' – he pronounced it, 'Thenk'.

'I would like . . . *Mein Fuhrer*, I want to have your baby.'

He recoiled slightly, said, 'Oh la la!', smiled, disentangled his hand from hers, shrugged at Frau Walter who was mumbling apologies, and completed his circuit of the room.

As Frau Walter left the house, after observing the proprieties, she snapped at Magda: 'You have embarrassed me.'

They climbed into the car.

Magda said: 'I couldn't help myself.'

'It was not good behaviour, you have taken advantage of my kindness.'

'I'm sorry, but I meant what I said.'

'That is no excuse.'

Magda cried, she blubbed huge tears inelegantly.

Frau Walter said: 'I shall speak to my husband. We will see what can be done. Where is your handkerchief? The Wels shouldn't see you crying.'

Magda controlled herself as best she could, thanked and said goodbye to Frau Walter, said she had a splitting headache to Frau Wels, and retired to her bedroom – retired hurt, as was apt to happen to her cricket-playing brothers.

She spent another night in turmoil, and was plunged into a more intense state of tension, excitation, dread, and every other emotion – or so it seemed – the next morning. She had received a message from the Chancellor's secretariat to the effect that she was to meet Herr Doktor Waxmann at three o'clock that afternoon at a Nuremberg address.

The message reached her via Frau Walter, who must have spilled the beans effectively. Frau Wels was a discreet person, she presented a sympathetic face to Magda but asked no questions, and Magda offered no answers and again left the house as soon as possible. She spent the hours before her appointment in picture galleries and parks, jumping to various conclusions, the preferred one of which, preferred and disturbing, was that Dr Waxmann would lead her into the presence of Hitler.

At three o'clock she rang one of the seven doctors' bells on the door of an old-style house in a respectable neighbourhood. A female receptionist in a white coat invited her in and escorted her to a waiting room. Her heart beat too fast and loudly, but she was seized with incipient disappointment – where was Hitler? Dr Waxmann appeared, also wearing white, a white jacket. He was thirtyish, dark-haired, red-lipped, had good teeth and spoke English. He was polite and smiled at her. He ushered her into his consulting room – a couch was half-hidden by a curtain in the corner. They faced each other across a desk, and he spoke good-humouredly of his English nanny, his years at Oxford, his affection for English people and English women in particular – 'I wish to tickle them and make them happy.'

She interrupted him: 'Why am I here?'

'Ah yes, why indeed, a good question.'

'You see,' she proceeded, 'I thought, I hoped, I was hoping...'

'Ah yes,' he nodded. 'Yes, yes, that is no.' He laughed. 'So sorry, dear lady, to be an unworthy substitute. You are lucky though – our Chancellor has rejected your offer, and instructed me to offer you his gratitude and his regrets.'

'But I...' Magda began and choked on the words.

'Dear lady, attractive woman, if I may say so, let me be frank,' Dr Waxmann resumed in his silky voice. 'We are alone in this room and can speak freely. The object of your affections is an outstanding, even a unique, man, and that also applies to his *amours*. He is not satisfied with the conventional commerce between a man and a woman. He requires services from women that are repugnant to many. To render such services, as you seem to be willing to do, would not be good for you, in any sense, and you would know a dangerous secret. A young woman of my acquaintance who knew that secret and could have divulged it was disposed of. The danger was political.'

'What are you talking about?'

'The secret of our Chancellor's requirements in the embrace of Venus, and his difficulty in achieving an orgasm, would do him great damage in the eyes of the German people. The girl of my acquaintance knew too much and had another lesson to learn. She was shot.'

'Who by?'

'Her lover.'

'Oh no!'

'Herself, if you would prefer to think so.'

'No!'

The doctor shrugged his shoulders.

Magda said: 'All the same, all the same...'

'I have been ordered to tell you to go home. Our friend in the high place wishes it. And who am I to assist such a seductive young person to rebel and risk a bullet to the brain? Do not play with fire, Miss Magdalen. Germany today is a more foreign country than it used to be. You must practise philosophy.'

'I can't,' Magda sobbed.

He removed his spectacles.

'Lie on the couch, please. I will listen to your heart and try to find a remedy for your indisposition.'

She was amenable. His red lips might have warned her if she had not been thinking of other lips under a toothbrush moustache. She was soothed by his caresses. Anyway she did not care. She was as ready as he was, and if possible more impatient.

He was solicitous afterwards. Neither of them had anything to apologise for. She clung to him, and he referred to love. He wanted to meet again, the following day or night, but she said she had to do her packing. They parted with kisses that consoled and were still quite hungry.

The day after that she travelled back to Cornwall. At Castle Scar she was welcomed, then ticked off for having offended Cornelia, thanks to whom her whole family was aware of her interest in Adolf Hitler. She was cross-questioned by her siblings – it was like an inquisition; and she was reproached and scolded, in particular by her brother Noah, who had communist leanings. And when she felt honour bound to go and say sorry to Cornelia, the door of the cottage was not opened in response to her knocking although lights were on in the sitting-room.

Magda found herself on the verge of breakdown as a result of this sequence of novel, soul-searing, topsy-turvy, and finally depressing events.

Her weakness notwithstanding, she remembered that Hitler had prevailed against the odds, and was roused to defend him and herself.

49

Noah had led the charge against that clown, that barrackroom lawyer, that bandit chief with cut-throat tendencies, that disgrace to the human race with whom she was apparently infatuated. Brothers and sisters had chimed in with objections to his looks, the viciousness of his speechifying, his private army of hooligans, his reign of terror that had got him where he was, his maniacal loathing of Jews, and his militarism that meant war.

The most rational of her arguments was that he was powerful. Whatever his methods of electioneering, he had been elected Chancellor of Germany. The German nation, the German army, a majority of Germans adored him – at a Nazi rally she had seen and heard adoration in action, an outpouring of loyalty that was unknown in England, mass dedication to a leader and his will and his cause. All of it inspired her. Moreover, she had met and been charmed by him. She was convinced that he could, if he would, change the world in roughly the same ways proposed by the Band of Hope. He was a socialist, if a National Socialist, which might not be perfect but was better than some political allegiances.

For her, the crux of the matter was that she had perceived in Hitler the qualities that they – she and her siblings – must summon up in order to realise their ideals. High-flown sentiments and schemes, everything the eight of them had devised over the years, were chaff that the wind would blow away, water that would dry in the heat of the sun, without some of what Hitler was made of, without the power to convert theory into practice.

Yes, all right, she had fallen for him, she admitted, but he excited her because he was proof – seemed to prove – that their solutions to the problems of modernism were not necessarily pie in the sky. She had aspired to enlist him in their crusade, or at least receive his advice and encouragement. Think of how wonderful it would be if he were to borrow their ideas and try them out in his new Germany!

Nonsense, her siblings chorused repeatedly in reply.

Without preamble or warning Magda rested her case. The time came when she ceased to answer back. She had something else on her mind. She confessed – not to God, she dared not – she confessed to her mother.

Her circumstances forced her to do so. She was desperate – in 1934 an illegitimate baby in a family like hers meant trials and tribulations without end. She would have to verify her suspicions for better or worse. She had to see a doctor, the family doctor, Dr Hopkinson – she knew no other in England – and he would inform her parents, he would have to inform them. Meanwhile, she was unable to attend Mass, for, without confessing in the Catholic sense and telling the truth to Father O'Malley she was not entitled to commune with God. Her mother would notice if she missed a single Mass. Her mother was unavoidable – she had to be told before she discovered, and only she could help with the visit to Dr Hopkinson.

Magda was pregnant.

Through a veil of tears, in the car with her mother, she announced her decisions – she did not have to ask permission, there was no valid alternative. She would go and talk to the father of the child. He was called Waxmann – she did not know his first name.

Mary tried but failed to persuade her daughter not to be hasty. At Castle Scar, as instructed, she collected a small suitcase already packed, also Edward, while Magda waited in the car. They then drove to the station by way of a bank, and waited together for the train to London. Their goodbyes were painful.

Dr Waxmann was not married. Luckily he was a Catholic, and he offered to marry Magda and she accepted – his Christian name was Heinrich. The wedding was celebrated in Germany with minimum delay. The bride was given away by her father – she had insisted that only her parents should attend, she wanted no members of The Band of Hope. In due course a baby boy, Fritz, was born.

Edward Penzoote again spoke to Jones, this time in the garden of Castle Scar – they were attending to the roses.

'I don't think Magda's story's had a happy ending.'

'Sorry about that,' Jones replied.

'And things could get a lot worse than they are.'

'Oh ah!'

'She chose to think Hitler was not too different from her brothers and sisters. She wants one of them to be another Hitler.'

'Does she now!'

'How she could beats me.'

'Well, she's clever, sir – they all are.'

'That's the trouble.'

WINIFRED

She was called Winnie. She was more of a Winnie than a Winifred. She seemed to be nothing like her elder sister Magdalen. Magda was always a big girl, Winnie verged on *petite*, had curly blonde instead of straight brown hair, a plump elastic sort of body and dimples. The differences did not stop there. Magda was respected, Winnie was fun. Magda had deep feelings, Winnie was shallow. Magda was moral, at least she was stronger on religion.

Resemblances existed nevertheless. They were both Hopes. They were like each other and their siblings in that they were rebels, reformers, who presumed to think they knew better than the rest of us.

Winnie had no patience with Magda's long-drawn-out virginity. Virginity was all very well, but only as part of the armoury of the war of the sexes. Her own attitude to love was as frivolous as Magda's was serious. She lived to be loved, and she had the resources that enabled her to obtain it. Perhaps it was admiration rather than true love that she was born to need.

It had been obvious in her cradle. She won the competition for favour in the nursery. She was popular with the boys at her first school, not the other girls. Her childhood was the cocoon. Aged ten or eleven the butterfly fluttered out of it.

In the higher tides of the sea below the Scar, she played longer than her sisters and brothers with the youths from the village. And when the sea was out, she made a point of being the one who was chased across the ribbed sands in games of French and English. She had the beginnings of a womanly figure before she was a woman, bathing suits suited her, and she looked prettier than ever in swimming-caps and sun-hats. All her followers were rewarded with smiles, meaningful glances, teasing pushes, tickles underwater, and banter on the beach: commitments were not on the menu.

The path to the Castle wound upwards by zig-zagging, and she formed almost a habit of looking down in a certain sweet way at the youth or more often youths who were looking up. She paused and her eyes met other eyes, she rounded the U-turn and again made the ocular promises she would not keep. She was so young, so innocent! Edward, if he happened to catch sight of her from above or below, would shake his head as if to scold her. Her siblings sometimes criticised her for leading the youths a dance, but she took no notice, she did not care – she was not a careful person.

Exceptionally, she went through no ugly phase. At seventeen she was ready to conquer on a field of battle larger than the Penzoote beach. She met a boy called Tim. She pinned a red poppy on to the lapel of his tweed jacket, she was selling poppies in remembrance of the Great War in Penzoote village high street. She knew at once he was in her web, she could feel the little tug that told her he was caught. He smiled at her and she smiled back.

'Do you live near here?' he asked.

'Yes, Castle Scar,' she replied. 'Do you?'

'Yes, at Trepenison. I bicycled over to see what was going on at Penzoote.'

'Well – now you know.'

'I'm Tim Wickenden.'

'I'm Winnie Hope.'

'How do you do?'

'Very well, thank you.'

They laughed.

The consequence was that Tim invited her to tea and tennis at the Wickenden home in Trepenison, the Old Rectory. She met his father and mother, his sister Angela, who was not so good-looking as her brother, and two other contemporaries, Sheila and Bobby, unrelated friends, and spent a happy afternoon – she was the prettiest girl there. She liked Tim, but he was still an undergraduate at Oxford. Besides, Angela said something that took her mind off Tim. Angela revealed that she was soon to be dragged up to London to attend Queen Charlotte's ball for debutantes.

'Mummy's taking me – I won't know a soul – and I don't want to be in society – who'll feed my pets while I'm doing the season?'

Angela was talking to Winnie, they had been playing a doubles against Tim and Bobby. The girls were friends already – Angela was not vain or competitive.

'I don't know about that ball,' Winnie said.

Angela explained she would have to wear a white ballgown, and curtsy to royalty, and thereupon would be eligible to be asked to all the posh parties thrown by the parents of the other debutantes, at which matches were meant to be made.

'It's a marriage market, and I think it's squalid,' Angela said.

'Could I come too?' Winnie asked.

The plan worked well from Winnie's point of view. Edward and Mary gave the senior Wickendens permission to 'bring out' their daughter. Winnie was also 'dragged' to the Wickendens' rented house in London and in Angela's wake to social engagements. By the middle of the season she had shaken off Angela, and moved in with a less strait-laced young ladyship who belonged in a smarter set.

She and Antonia Burgess were flatmates for months that stretched into years. Winnie augmented her allowance from her father by modelling and taking old ladies to the cinema, while Antonia got jobs as receptionist in car show-rooms. They became nocturnal, lived their lives after dark, came to life when the sun went down. It was cocktail and dinner parties, dances and night clubs, dallying with boys who would be boys and fighting off older men, risking their virtue and having narrow squeaks. In spite of hangovers and wondering where the next meal was coming from, it was a giggle. Winnie was a 'bright young thing', a member of the group so-called by the gossip columnists, and mixed with the *demi-monde* on the outskirts of respectability. They wore disguises, gate-crashed, behaved outrageously, played practical jokes, organised treasure hunts in the West End, took photographs of one another in white wigs or a few feathers, and announced privately and publicly that at any rate they were not roundheads or squaretoes, and never bores.

Winnie and Antonia agreed that, on occasions, each would like to have the flat to themselves for a couple of hours. But this was not yet the age of lust. And Magda's tragi-comical slip-up was exemplary, a memo of the laws writ large by infant hands and enforced by etiquette and the conventions. Winnie clung on to what she called her principles, even if in practice they were repeatedly strained not far from breaking-point.

She did not go home in the period in question. There was always a reason not to be good, nor to do things that ought to be done.

The party in the Public Baths in the North London suburb of Green Heath was an instance of the above. The invitations were received three months before it happened, and from then on all other priorities were put in the shade. The party giver was a Peruvian moneybag with a long name that everybody reduced to one word, Arturo. The recommended dress was beachwear and diamonds. The venue caused much discussion: Winnie and some of her cronies went to spy out the land and were put off by the grim Edwardian monstrosity, the smell of chemicals, the dirty-looking water and the ear-splitting acoustics. But rumours counteracted such impressions and suspicions. Arturo was going to spend a fortune on changing the face of the place. He was employing the interior decorators that were in vogue, he would be employing the best bands, the most scrumptious of caterers, and half the Metropolitan Police Force.

The time of year was December. Winnie and Antonia decided to go in swimsuits and dressing-gowns of brightly coloured warm material. They bought gaudy brooches of fake precious stones, diamonds included – Arturo owned diamond mines, let him and his family wear the real ones! They were invited separately to dine here and there before the 'bathing' do – the first syllable of 'bathing' pronounced like the city of Bath – began at ten p.m.

It was a cold night, cold, dark and drizzling. The neighbourhood of the baths in Green Heath was *terra incognita* for the partygoers – residential property that looked like seaside lodgings, ribbon development of run-down shops, an ill-lit high street, and council offices including the leisure centre. Everyone scuttled in between two lines of a few jeering onlookers. But inside, through the doors held open by liveried staff, it was a warm wonderland of magic and money.

The pool was blue and illuminated by

underwater lights. The ceiling above was a new installation, painted to resemble the night sky with stars twinkling through. The former tea room had become a dance floor edged with banks of flowers. A band already played on a stage where the tea urns had stood on counters. There was a huge bar at the other end of the hall, and tables and chairs scattered amongst palm trees and softly lit. On either side of the pool were changing rooms, doors open, day-beds visible, all repainted in bright colours. The echo had been done away with.

Arturo wore a white tuxedo, his wife a black dress and tiara, daughters in swimsuits with brooches and bangles, a son in a diamond necklace. Guests were welcomed informally with smiles and waves of the hand – not many guests had ever set eyes on the host and vice versa. Outdoor overcoats were being deposited in changing rooms, and ladies emerged in a variety of unladylike and usually unflattering costumes and laughed at one another. The men wore more or less tight trunks – shy ones immediately dived into the water, which was heated to blood-heat. The whole area above water was baking hot. The embarrassment of attire was mitigated by the drinks that waiters were offering persuasively – Winnie downed one, it looked like a special brand of champagne, it had a brown tinge, and was extraordinarily delicious.

Winnie was another sort of star from the word go. Physical defects passed muster more easily on a beach than in a ballroom with pool adjoining:

her perfect figure as well as her face attracted attention. Other bright young things joined the party, horse-play began, and Winnie was relieved of her dressing-gown and swung into the water. She swam like a mermaid and gained more plaudits. Lots of people swam, then dried themselves in the cubicles, donned another bathing-dress they had brought along or chose a new one from a huge selection in the cloakrooms, fortified themselves with another little drink, and took to the dance floor.

Winnie danced and swam and danced again. She had suitors trying to dance or to swim with her, she had difficulty in keeping them out of the cubicle she used. Everybody was getting excited, the dance music was accompanied by screams and squeals, the non-stop circulation of that champagne probably accounted for action in the cubicles, cries of 'Isn't it fun!' merged with female admonitions, 'Stop it, don't you dare, get off me!' A man informed Winnie that the champagne was a champagne cocktail, it had brandy, sugar and angostura bitters added and was double-strength; and she began to realise she might have drunk more than was good for her.

At some later stage barrels were wheeled on to the dance floor. They were bran tubs, full of presents, jewel boxes containing jewellery, gold bangles, wristwatches, cufflinks of sapphires and rubies, diamonds galore. There was a mad dash to grab the presents. One of Winnie's suitors sat her down at the bar, saying she was not up to the bun-fight round the tubs, he would do the dirty work and dig in on her behalf. He was as good as his word, he brought her a butterfly brooch made of platinum and precious stones. She thanked him with an embrace that became closer, he commented on her wet swimsuit, supported her into a cubicle, undressed and, as she put it afterwards, took advantage of her.

She got rid of him. She accepted another drink to steady herself. She had lost her virginity on a previous occasion, a singular regrettable event. She had rushed to a doctor, obtained nullifying treatment, also the insertion of a permanent and apparently foolproof contraceptive device. She was nonetheless worried, accepted more drinks, swam to try to sober herself, and another suitor rescued her in one sense and endangered her in another. In the small hours a game was invented and played. Men pushed the girls about on the wet and slippery poolside tiles. Then some girls full of Dutch courage were prevailed upon to remove their swimsuits so that they would slide farther on the tiles – they were made to sit doubled up, and were 'bowled' the length of the pool and back again. Winnie played the game and as a result was a third unlucky time in a cubicle.

She locked the cubicle door after shoving number three out, lay down on the couch and sank into sleep or a trance.

She came to in daylight. She found her dressing-gown and present, also some drunken revellers revelling no more, refused the offer of a lift in a strange man's car, left the premises and in the grubby street was stared at by hostile plebeians in raw winter weather. After a long walk and a long wait at a bus stop, where she was again exposed to adverse scrutiny and comment, she caught a series of buses crammed with the world's workers and arrived at last at her flat. Antonia, who had also been at the party, criticised her conduct there and said it would reflect badly on their friendship.

She had to seek alternative accommodation. She moved in with Gladys Milbow, an older unmarried acquaintance whom she had met at Mass. She was no longer a bright young thing, she was apprehensive and unhappy: more new experiences. She was soon sick of Gladys' company, and fled to Castle Scar, but was too restless to stay there, telling lies and dodging her mother and Father O'Malley. Back in London she shunned her former playmates and thought of throwing in her lot with Magda, Hans Waxmann and little Fritzi in Germany. When she finally dared to go to a doctor, her worst fears were confirmed.

She was spurred to take action for the sake of her baby and its surname. She reviewed her options and settled for the second of the three seducers at the Green Heath Baths. He was John Carrol, a City man, a rich man. John was single, fortyish, overweight, loud, pleased with himself, and might be kind. She contacted him, she made herself look as pretty as possible and went to his house in Chelsea. They were alone there, he was immediately amorous, and she cried on his shoulder. She spoke of his baby before anything else. He proposed, she accepted him, they sealed their engagement, he took her out to dinner, and that night and again in the morning she had to make contributions to the purchase of her solitaire engagement ring.

The marriage was a pyrrhic victory for Winnie. She counted the probable spoils of battle, her reputation repaired, a father for her child, a roof in Chelsea over their heads, and further additions to her collection of jewellery. On the other hand she was defeated or at least deflated. She had never been attracted by John Carrol. She discovered she did not even like him, and insisted on a civil wedding not only because it would be quieter, but also because it would not count in the Roman Catholic context. He was not popular at Castle Scar. She had to submit to demeaning tasks to stop him harming the unborn baby on their honeymoon. He was flush with money and pettily mean in small ways. Her friends disapproved of him, and vice versa, and she hated his cronies. She also hated his golf, bridge, gluttony and materialism, while he complained of her flirting and foolishness.

A few months before giving birth she refused to recognise his marital rights, and a few weeks later she found him in their marital bed with two naked girls. She had returned from a visit to Castle Scar earlier than expected, and she sued for divorce. She received it without delay because of her condition and because John was the guilty party; but she was paid off with peanuts – her phrase for the financial settlement. His team of lawyers revealed the circumstances in which conception occurred and cast doubt on the child's paternity; the judge was a man at once sanctimonious and sorry for the sexual starvation of the defendant; and, according to Winnie, she was the victim of a beastly male conspiracy.

The baby was a boy. She called him Peter, and mentioned his surname as infrequently as possible. She was not maternal. She fancied men, not miniature boys. She required assistance with Peter, a nanny, who would cost more than her alimony could afford. She booked an appointment with a fashionable gynaecologist and paid the ruinous price of an interior contraceptive device that was guaranteed not to betray her. She then sought a meeting with the first man who had made free with her at Arturo's party. He was William Nevershot, a Norfolk farmer with some social pretensions – he had bumbled along in pursuit of one bright young thing after another. He was in his thirties, small and stocky, and said by Winnie's smart pals to have permanent manure on his shoes. He came down to London to visit her one evening in her dingy flat. She introduced him to Peter.

As they looked at the infant in his cot, Winnie said to William: 'He's yours.'

William broke out in a sweat. He asked for whisky – she gave him cooking brandy. She explained that Peter was a child of the cubicle, and that she had never known any love affair to compare with William's virile performance in so unlikely a setting. Her problem had been, her reason for not contacting William before was, that she happened to be engaged to marry John Carrol at the time and had felt obliged to keep her word. It was such a silly muddle, she said – loving one man and marrying another! Her marriage to John Carrol was a charade, she said, he was a sex maniac, but, she added, she had always thought of William while she was with John. Anyway, John had been unfaithful to her with prostitutes, two prostitutes simultaneously, and at last she had liberated herself from his clutches. As for Peter, throughout the sorrows of her first marriage she had hoped and believed that William would recognise the fruit of his loins, although she herself was an independent person and was glad to be a free agent again.

The long and short of it was a proposition acceded to when a proposal was forthcoming.

Poor Mrs Nevershot was no better off than Mrs Carrol had been. Winnie had failed to feather her nest by means of marriage to John Carrol, in her innocence she had not stood up for herself, and allowed him to get away with financial murder. She resolved to rectify matters; but William said that as she brought him no dowry he was not handing over a lump sum for goods on approval. William was more of a beast than John had been, judging by manners. He was agricultural in all respects. His farmhouse was old-fashioned, he had warned her: she found it primitive. Norfolk was muddy and its east wind intolerable. Her husband was boringly absent for hours of every day and boringly present otherwise.

She had too many headaches to suit him, and he complained of her behaving like a bitch out of season. After mere months of matrimony the only climax that meant anything to her was a great row, her accusing him of being a dolt and a barbarian, him causing her grievous bodily harm, a dislocated jaw and deafness in one ear – in short, grounds for divorce. Winnie sued, William cross-petitioned, the court case was ugly and public, Arturo's party was described in detail, and this judge, evidently an inverted snob as well as a chauvinist, ruled that the wife's aristocratic relatives could look after her and her child, and extended sympathy to the husband.

Winnie returned to Cornwall. She was ashamed of her behaviour, mortified by her matrimonial mistakes, and nearly bankrupt. She had explaining to do and apologies to make to her parents and siblings. She had deadly sins to confess to Father O'Malley.

Absolution and pardon were cemented by permission to live in a cottage in the village of Penzoote, part of the Castle Scar estate. Gradually Winnie recovered her health and confidence, although never her baby-doll looks. The scandal subsided. The assertive genes of an inactive member of the Band of Hope stirred.

Winnie had a cause, the cause of her experience, and now she embraced that with the novelty of passion. Men were lustful, selfish, irresponsible, and their part in the act of procreation lasted two or three minutes; women were the mothers of the race, their pregnancies lasted nine months, and they were infinitely more responsible for the welfare of their offspring than fathers were. Yet in the eyes of judges presiding over divorce courts, male judges, men were the rich lords of creation and women the beggar maids. The divorce laws emphasised the right of a man to keep his money and the wrong of a woman to demand some of it. The wrong she was keen to right was the divorce law. She thought it favoured husbands at the expense of wives. She had not got what she thought she deserved and would have liked to obtain from her two husbands, and she converted her resentment into a hobby horse. She lectured her siblings in her turn. Infidelity and physical violence did not automatically entitle the wives on the receiving end to a share of the husband's wealth, he did not have to pay for his pleasure in that sense; whereas wives who strayed from the straight and narrow, even retrospectively, as in Winnie's own case, were punished by being condemned to penury.

Winnie pleaded that no outsider ever knew exactly how equivalent a sexual relationship was, if the pleasure of it was equal, how good or how bad it was for each, and for how long, therefore statistics were unobtainable and guesses were almost certainly unjust. Judges were old and out of touch with the sexual mores of the young. Judges probably had chosen to marry judicially and had no knowledge or understanding of divorce. And politicians were the worst law-makers, beside the point as it was to say so.

Anyway, Winnie had the ideal at her fingertips

– she was not a Hope for nothing. Divorce should be simplified in accordance with practicality and common sense. In the event of the break-up of a true or formal relationship between consenting adults, marriage in particular, family funds should be split fifty-fifty.

And divorce should be obtainable on demand – no more red tape, no more guilt.

She should have received half the value of John Carrol's house in Chelsea and his portfolio of shareholdings, and again half of William Nevershot's farm, farmhouse and capital. The future she envisaged would recognise the responsibilities of love and sex, and legalise the principle of fair pay for fair play in the sexual context; and she compared it with the mere gratuities, tips, she had been given by her two wealthy husbands, not nearly enough money to pay for the life she was accustomed to by birth, nor for the education of her son, whomsoever his father might be.

These proposals of hers provoked noisy debates and arguments at Castle Scar. Winnie compromised to the extent of allowing that a poor male partner should be able to claim half the fortune of a rich female one; but that was only to reinforce her forecast that one day both parties to a sexual union would have to share equally their combined material resources if or when they parted for good. She rebutted the charge that such a law would spell the end of marriage in all its forms, also of love relationships and the upbringing of children by a father and mother

– she denied that she was advocating sexual satisfaction by one-night stands. She enlisted in a feminist 'action' group named *Who Rules The World?*, and occasionally waved a placard outside the Houses of Parliament.

Edward found peace in the company of Jones.

One evening by the picket fence he informed his gardener: 'They're on about divorce.'

'That'll be Miss Winnie,' Jones responded.

'She wants divorce made easy, and couples who can't stick together splitting their money.'

'Oh ah?'

'She's advising us to expect to be fleeced by anybody we go to bed with.'

'When's it going to happen?'

'Some time never.'

'What do you think, sir?'

'Good business for some, bad business for the rest of us.'

'There'd be a lot of wickedness.'

'Yes – more wickedness – my children aren't worried about the wickedness – they don't believe in evil.'

'Well, they haven't been in a war.'

'Not yet.'

NOAH

Noah Hope was a cradle Catholic and a convert to communism. He had been converted by the bourgeois dons at university, who had taught him that a cull of class enemies – such as the bourgeoisie, oddly enough – would create heaven on earth. He had been a good boy, but slow – he was an enthusiastic angler. A metaphor drawn from angling described his politics: he had swallowed communism hook, line and sinker. He turned against the god of his childhood, his parents' God, and worshipped Lenin – he preferred Lenin to Stalin because Lenin had an upper class background like Noah himself. He did post-graduate studies in Russian language and literature and won a doctorate.

He had lagged behind his brothers and sisters, and now proved he was not stupid. He seemed to gain confidence by identifying with his comrades in the largest country in the world, soon to become the strongest. In Magda's absence in Germany, he seized his chance to rail against her hero, Adolf Hitler, in the approved vocabulary of the Bolsheviks: Hitler was a slimy cockroach, fit only to be ground into the dust, a dunghill, a cancerous tumour, a piece of poisonous ordure.

His mother objected to his bad language, nobody liked it, therefore Noah was gratified to think he had broken loose from his family, from that class which the Bolsheviks said deserved to be liquidated. He was a terrible inverted snob, he snarled at privilege, affected boorish behaviour, ate his meals in the kitchen with the cook instead of in the dining-room, and said the Penzootes' way of life was a shameful anachronism: none of which stopped him sending out job applications on writing paper printed with his name plus both his titles – Doctor The Honourable Noah Hope.

Edward punctured the red balloon. He said Noah was not to live and luxuriate at Castle Scar and at the same time call its owners who paid the bill he was running up 'rotten ... rotting rotters'. He said Noah was advertising the ugly aspect of the new rulers of Russia. He also suggested that Noah might do better and feel more at home on the steppes than in the best location Cornwall had to offer.

Noah mended his ways. He reverted to what he had been before he was brainwashed by the intellectuals who were convinced that they would do better than most in their brave new egalitarian state. His nature was kind, it was his kindness that made him susceptible to communism's claim to be on the side of the downtrodden. He thought of going to Russia, even living there, as urged by his father.

His participation in the chatter of the siblings was more reasonable. He granted that Magda's commitment to Nazism and his to communism were linked inasmuch as both he and his sister saw that however good their ideas, ideals, aims and projects were, they were simply hot air without the power to implement them. Lenin and Hitler had seized power, and they were reforming their nations. Power was the engine that could drive the best-laid plans made at Castle Scar into the realm of possibility.

He also modified his criticism of Winnie's marital adventures. He attempted to console her by relating that marriage was discouraged in the USSR, would soon be banned, and that the children of heterosexual affairs were raised in orphanages. As for her thought that the combined fortunes of lovers calling it a day should be divided equally, he could support it since it redistributed wealth, which he was dead against.

Incidentally, Winnie did not point out that he was misunderstanding her, she did not like to say that she would not have been averse to receiving more of her husbands' money – avarice was not a feature of the futuristic landscape of the Band of Hope.

Noah spent time in London ostensibly to get a job. In fact, he got a visa to enter the USSR. He had queued for it at Russian diplomatic offices for four and a half months. He eventually persuaded hard-faced Russian apparatchiks that he was a supporter of the achievements and ambitions of the hierarchy of government by and for the *moujiks*, not a capitalist spy and wrecker. He had been body-searched umpteen times because of carrying his fisherman's basket full of his home-made fishing flies into the Consulate of the Embassy in order to prove that he only wanted to catch a few bolshevik fish.

He was as excited as his phlegmatic temperament could be. His firm conviction was that, while his siblings forecast a future that would be horrible if their advice was not heeded, he was actually going to where the future had begun and an improved world was spinning into shape. His sisters half-believed him, his brothers asked for postcards from paradise, his mother gave him medicaments and advice about keeping warm in a frigid land, and his father said to him: 'Remember, generals also have a strategy for retreat.'

The rest of Noah's story was told in his own words in letters he wrote to all at Castle Scar.

'A frustrating time so far,' the first letter ran. 'It has taken me ten days to travel from Cornwall to where I write from. I have already wasted three of my fourteen-day permits to reside in the USSR. My train was held up for twenty-four hours at the Russian border, largely because of me, I gathered, and then I was arrested when I reached Tula. The basic cause of my delays and, frankly, ill-treatment, was the assassination in December of Kirov, a top politician. The newspapers are still full of it, and the whole country seems to be having a nervous breakdown. Sergei Kirov was the big noise in Leningrad, St Petersburg of yore, he was Stalin's heir apparent and tremendously popular. The assassin has been caught but the papers say other people were pulling his strings. In the end, the authorities in Tula released me – thank goodness my Russian isn't too rusty! The next difficulty was where I would be allowed to lay my head – the hotel I was booked into in Tula was out of bounds. At midday today I was driven out here to a village called Orla and a cottage of the meanest type.

'I am not complaining. I have made my bed, as the saying goes. The weather is colder than Cornwall's ever was. Spring here is not spring-like by our standards. Snow covered the steppes I saw from the train, and the snow that was melting in Orla this afternoon is freezing again. Stalactites are daggers of ice barring my tiny window. At least my dwelling is not on the steppes, which are intolerably big, empty and boring.

'Orla must resemble the so-called villages for serfs that are referred to by Tolstoy and Chekhov. Primitive bungaloid structures, they would be outhouses for farm machinery or chicken sheds in England, are scattered irregularly on either side of a road with deep cart-tracks. Cattle are probably kept indoors at this time of year. This afternoon chickens were pecking about and a dog barked at the ancient Ford rattle-trap taxi that brought me out from Tula. A forest of silver birches surrounds the village – men carrying axes and saws, wearing peasant clothing, mostly sackcloth apparently, were emerging through the trees at the end of a day's work round about five o'clock. The word is that pools full of fish are located in amongst the trees.

81

'I am a lodger in the habitation of Pavel and Marfa – "paying guest" would be to call a sow's ear a silk purse! I have been told the patronymics of my hosts, the names of the men of whom they are son and daughter, but I can't remember them and could not spell them – no matter. They are not young and not old, they are ageless small Russian dumplings with Asian eyes, pink cheeks and big unrelenting smiles. They seem not to be workers of the world, they may be retired, or maybe their business is to take in one lodger at a time. Their home is primitive to a shocking extent – it shocked me at any rate. It's croft-size, made of logs and mud, roofed with turf, and consists of one room, a stove with complex chimney, and a lean-to slip of a room, which is mine. The chimney is covered with plaster or baked mud, and has a kink in the middle creating a shelf on which Pavel and Marfa sleep under huge feather quilts. My bed is another shelf alongside the chimney, which gives out a little heat. I lie on it as I write to you by the light of a peculiar candle – tallow? – more like a night-light, wax in a shallow dish – not good for the eyes. The lavatory is out of doors, a hole in the ground partly concealed by waist-high wattle – down to earth with a vengeance.

'My evening meal was cabbage soup with some unidentified protein floating in it and stale bread like a rusk. I cannot understand Pavel's Russian, it's mutual, we converse by means of smiles and sighs – Marfa is not a communicator, let alone a talker.

'I'd better stop now and try to get warm in bed. I'm really glad to be in the USSR, but the truth is I have not received much of a welcome so far. Russians certainly excel in showing you that you're not wanted.

'Please prepare yourself for more long letters! Unless the fish are more friendly than the local plebs, I'll have nothing to do in this God-forsaken backwater for the next ten days except to write to you.'

The second letter was not so long.

'Two difficult days – and nights! My first night here, after I had finished my other unposted letter, was disturbed by the inharmonious snores of Pavel and Marfa. We were at close quarters, almost in the same bed, separated only by a few planks, and repeatedly I was convinced that one or other or perhaps both had died, an ominous silence of half a minute or so had fallen, and then a cracker of a snore would warn me that death had not had mercy on me – they were alive and would rock me awake on my shelf until morning.

'That was at five o'clock – dawn with cocks crowing and movement next door. Breakfast was a sort of gruel, more cabbage soup with breadcrumbs added and more tea, herbal tea that tasted like dishwater. After breakfast I indicated my bristly chin and was eventually given a small bowl of hot water – not enough to shave in – I used it for ablutions, and resolved not to bother to shave during my holiday – Pavel is unshorn. When I put on outdoor clothing and prepared my fishing gear, Marfa also gave me food, a slab of hard bread and some slices of onion.

'My day's fishing was a bit tragic. The weather was foul, cloudy with strong wind from the north. The pool or lake to which I have been directed was two hours' walking distant from Orla. And I was followed by adults and children, a small crowd from nowhere. I caught two tiny fish in four hours, walked back to the village, and, as soon as I had swallowed my cabbage soup, went to bed and to sleep – I was dog-tired and distressed.

'Today, my second day at the lake, was disturbing in another way. I suspected that the crowd, mostly of children but including some adults, was keeping me under surveillance. And no sooner had that idea crossed my mind than I noticed two men in suits and trilby hats undoubtedly watching my every move.

'No paranoia – my suspicions did not drop out of the blue. Pavel and Marfa pretend not to understand my most clearly articulated common phrases of the Russian language – it must be pretence and they must be under orders from someone not to converse with me. Moreover, I had with me Tolstoy's tract *What shall we do then?* – a title that could be the war-cry of my brothers, sisters and self – and I showed it to my hosts. They shook their heads, smiling, although my copy is in the original Russian. Maybe they are just illiterate. But I spoke to them of Lenin and Stalin, and my admiration of the revolutionaries of 1917, and again they smiled – who do they think I am, a menace or a lunatic?'

The third letter was dramatic.

'Oh dear!' it began. 'Days have passed and I have lost track of dates. I think I mentioned men in dark suits who were watching me. The day after that, when I returned to Orla, a black limousine was parked outside Pavel and Marfa's cott. It was a Russian car, it had curtains across the rear windows. And there was a smaller black car parked fifty yards along the roadway, and two men in trilbys stood by it, smoking – surely the two who had shadowed me before. I must admit I was apprehensive, having concluded that the cars and their occupants were waiting for me. In spite of my repudiation of harmful gossip to the effect that the USSR is a police state, I was frightened.

'The doors of the limousine opened. A tough guy stepped out of the front passenger seat and an army officer out of the back. The latter was tall, slim, authoritative and spoke English fluently.

'He said: "Good afternoon, sir. Apologies for detaining you. I wonder if you could spare me a few minutes of your time? We could talk in my car – it's warm in there."

'I complied. I had asked what I was meant to do with my fishing-rod etc, and he issued an order to the tough guy who immediately took charge of it all. The back part of the interior of the limousine, behind the glass partition, was spacious and luxurious – the engine clanked away and powered the heating apparatus. We were alone, side by side on the back seat.

'He was – he is – a charming chap, a polite gentleman, called me sir and Mr Hope, and asked me to call him by his Russian first name, Fedor. He told me his mother had been English, his father was involved in government business, and he was a career soldier now on guard duty at the Kremlin in Moscow. He knew all about me, my membership of the Communist Party, my enthusiasm for the cause. He spoke drily, perhaps ambiguously, and came to the point, which was, in short, would I do the USSR a great favour? It would entail one night in the Kremlin or possibly two nights. Comrade Stalin was aware of the request that he – Fedor – was making. No harm to me was anticipated. I could become a hero of the USSR, a great distinction. My cooperation would be of historical importance.

'My question, what was the favour, could not be answered for the time being, he told me: I would have to trust him, trust Comrade Stalin, and the integrity of the politics and politicians I support.

'Of course I agreed, I was flattered while my knees knocked together. I was flattered and curious, flattered and alarmed.

'We drove to Moscow. The hours of the journey passed pleasantly enough, thanks to his soothing talk of literature, Russian and English, and a supply of little glasses of vodka – a lot of vodka in the little glasses.

'Night fell, Moscow was almost blacked out owing to lack of electricity, the Kremlin was all checkpoints and sentries, and we entered by an unassuming door in the dark, and climbed an ill-lit steep staircase. I was led into a modest living-room, part of a flat – my quarters. Fedor said food would be brought to me, and he would be able to tell me more in the morning.

'Sorry about the length of this letter – you'll soon see why it's long.

'Yes, the next morning, whenever that was, I was told that I would be required to double for Stalin, believe it or not!

'The reasons why Stalin needed a double, and how and why the choice of me had been confirmed overnight, remained hazy. I got it into my head later that Stalin himself had seen me without my knowing it, on that staircase somehow, or by a peephole into my flat, and approved. Anyway, they – Fedor with other men in attendance – again asked me to cooperate. I volunteered in fear and trembling, but quite willingly, for the cause, and because it will be for no more than two days.

'One of Fedor's attendants was a barber. He shaved my beard and dyed my hair and moustache. Another was a dentist, he shaped one of my front teeth, painlessly, thank God. A third was a tailor. Fedor had asked me not to speak to these three men, or to the person who carries trays of food. He spoke of discretion, he meant secrecy – I was a secret – what an adventure!

'Fedor left me at midday and said he would be back at eight. I ate a tasty lunch, and settled down to write to all of you.

'I now add a postscript.

'At eight Fedor arrived with the tailor and a complete khaki uniform such as I had seen Stalin wearing in photographs. Fedor informed me I was now to move into Stalin's own apartment. While changing my clothes my nerve failed me. Earlier in the day I had discovered that the door of my flat was locked. I brought to Fedor's attention my fear that I was a prisoner and had been kidnapped. He laughed at me. I had mistaken care for my safety for detention, he said. Nothing had been done against my will, he reminded me. But what would happen once I was in Stalin's attire, in Stalin's rooms? Nothing, Fedor replied. He then said it was already too late for me to change my mind.

'I was scared, but had to leave it at that. I mentioned my letters home, and Fedor told me to bring them along, he would arrange for them to reach England in one way or another.

'He then made a speech, praising my courage, loyalty and so on. I'm not boasting, I think he saw how unhappy I was and paid me compliments that might prop me up and give me Dutch courage.'

Noah's fourth letter was the last.

'My dearest parents and brothers and sisters, I think of you with tears in my eyes.

'I cannot conceal from you that my life is in ruins. It would be more manly to grin and bear catastrophe, but I cannot. Forgive me! I'll try to write the story, though my hand will shake.

'I moved into Stalin's rooms, his austere sitting-room, his study that contains his medium-sized desk, his wooden-seated chair and several other chairs, and his bedroom with the single bed – rooms beyond were inaccessible. To sit there, to sleep in that bed, gave me the heeby-jeebies. What on earth had I agreed to?

'In the morning of the next day, Fedor coached me in faking Stalin's writing, his initials that he used to sanction various papers, orders, laws and so on. I jibbed at that, but Fedor said a top civil servant would be bringing correspondence that had to be initialled – both the man and the initials were unavoidable. I was too deep in not to be deeper – I practised the Russian JS in the handwriting of Stalin, who had been educated and prepared for priesthood in a seminary. We rehearsed my conduct that would have to deceive the official.

'He arrived at seven o'clock. I sat at Stalin's desk, Fedor stood beside me, the only light in the room was the green-shaded desk-light – my face was in shadow and I pretended to be writing. The official greeted me and placed about ten sheets of paper on my desk. They were covered with lists of names. Fedor handed me a pen, and I wrote JS at the bottom of page one, then on the other pages. I reshuffled the pages, so that the first page was on top of the pile, and I read the heading. It was one word, not even in caps, it was: "execution".

'I froze. Fedor said something, and I flicked to another page on which I had noticed a different heading. The heading was: "camp". Fedor spoke again. I made a gesture that was intended to be negative – no, go away, stop, I won't, but it was misinterpreted, Fedor handed the sheaf of papers to the official and escorted him to the door.

'The game was over. Horrible explanations followed. Enlightenment was torture. I, who have always been anti capital punishment, against the shedding of blood, a humanist and a pacifist, I had signed the death warrants of hundreds, and sent hundreds to perish in Siberian prisons. I cried – Fedor cried, too. He hushed me and spoke into my ear: it was routine, he said. The USSR is governed by the cruellest oppression, he whispered. And I kept on crying for those poor people I had condemned to death, and because I had been gulled, because I had been an idiot. The high ideals of communism boiled down to bullying and murder, and I had been the silliest of asses to think well of politicians who could kill a king and his family in a cellar.

'How can I blame Fedor? He was more miserable than me. He had looked like a gent, a stuffed shirt, a diplomat of distinction, and he was weeping secretively. He was so sorry for having tricked me; but, he whispered in my ear, they had his wife and children, they would kill his family or send them to Siberia, which is another death sentence, if he failed to persuade me to participate in their charade. He referred to Kirov – the assassin of Kirov was Stalin, he hissed – no one was safe – Russia had become a slaughterhouse.

'And what was it, their charade? The aim could not be to get me to sign death warrants. Fedor reminded me that tomorrow would be the first of May. In England girls used to dance round maypoles on the first of May, in the USSR armed soldiers and tanks threaten the populace and the rest of the world. How and why was I involved in the parade? I was to stand and wave and salute the show – no need to speak to any of the other important people. What about the why? Stalin was sick.

'One other question: how much danger would I be in? Fedor promised, promised that he had been promised, swore on the heads of his son and daughter, that he would rescue me the moment the parade was over and drive me back to Orla, and I would be free to leave the USSR on the train on which I had a reserved seat on the next day.

'There it is – I have no alternative to doing as I am told – but I realise I am in danger – I know too much.

'My dearest parents, please accept my apologies for only honouring you as you deserve to be honoured belatedly. My siblings, forget my falsehoods! My God, forgive me for worshipping tyrants!

'P.S. It is the morning of Mayday and I have put on the army cap that will fool the people, as I have been fooled.'

On the second of May in Cornwall, at Castle Scar, Edward Penzoote read in his copy of *The Times* that an explosion had marred the military parade in Moscow, and wounded the Secretary-General of the Communist Party of the Soviet

Union, Joseph Stalin, who had been reviewing his troops. Stalin was carried away from the rostrum built above Lenin's tomb amidst public consternation, but he revived in a matter of minutes and was able to enhance his reputation as superman by returning to his rightful place to prolonged plaudits and cheering.

Edward, on reading the above, hoped that Noah was safe and well. When Noah did not return to England on the day he was expected, Edward began to worry, although he had heard of the unreliable old postal and telephonic systems in the USSR. Three months without a word from Noah almost convinced him that Noah was no more, although he spared Mary and their children his pessimistic opinion and continued to bang his head against the brick wall of lack of information from the Russian Embassy.

In the month of October a package arrived for Lord Penzoote. It was from Turkey, and it contained Noah's fishing gear and letters, also a piece of paper with one word on it: Fedor. The family read the letters sceptically, at first, then sadly. Edward supplied an explanatory commentary. His guesses were that Stalin needed a public relations boost because he was suspected of killing Kirov; that he or others plotted the explosion on Mayday; Fedor was bribed to lead the lamb to the slaughter by passports for himself and family enabling them to flee the USSR; in short, that everyone had lied, and that Noah's paradise was bloody hell.

Jones was told the story.

'Mr Noah, he didn't deserve to be blown up,'
Jones said.

'No.'

'I'm sorry, sir.'

'So am I,' Edward replied.

'He was a good lad.'

'Yes, but there are penalties for being wrong.'

'Oh ah!'

'My children wouldn't agree.'

PHILLIS

Phillis Hope was the fourth child of Edward and Mary Penzoote. She was so different from her siblings that they called her a changeling, a fairy child. She was fine-boned and dainty. She was painfully shy. Nothing was ever quite right for her, her clothes were uncomfortable, the parting of her hair was crooked, the dinner-table not laid neatly, it was the wrong day of the week. She suffered from perfectionism, and was chronically put out. The compensatory factor was her ethereal quality, her sweet patience considering her frustration.

She flitted through her childhood and even her youth. Her father compared her to a dragon fly, flashing through the family life, only alighting for a moment or two in a sunny spot; Mary corrected him, Phil was more like a humming bird. Neither description was very accurate. She was no dragon, and she failed to extract much honey from anywhere or anything. Perhaps she was a shadow of her parents, dancing light-footed after her father as he worked in the garden with Jones, or following her mother round the house, waiting to hug her or be hugged, or to touch her hand. It was the same with her brothers and sisters, she was their shadow, now this one now that, listening and watching, close and yet distant, laughing when they laughed, frowning and fleeing when they disagreed. She was a great favourite with the staff, they thought she was ladylike.

Her response to the Bible story, the prayers she was taught, and Father O'Malley's Bible Class, was wide-eyed. She was convinced, she was without scepticism. Gentle Jesus seemed to be related to Father Christmas in her psychology, and she believed she was called to be a handmaiden of the Almighty, who would protect her always. Her faith was touching and childish. When she began to sit alone in the chapel, and pray for too long on her knees at bedtime, Mary asked for advice from Father O'Malley, and he had to give her a talking-to.

'God isn't a magician,' he warned the girl.

'He's better than a magician,' she replied.

'Well, that's true, too, but...'

'Don't say I'm wrong to talk to Him, please, Father.'

'No, my dear, I won't, I couldn't, but you're only young once, you must enjoy yourself without delving deeply into religious matters. You can think deep thoughts later on.'

'Doesn't God do the thinking for me?'

'Yes, dear, but you have a good time while you can.'

Father O'Malley reported back to Mary that Phil was a good little girl, and there was no cause for alarm.

Her individuality was accentuated when she

was due to move from the village school to the Roman Catholic day-school for boys and girls aged eight or nine to seventeen or eighteen. Jones drove the three children older than Phil to and from the so-called Cornish Academy throughout term-time. Phil was expected to go with Magda, Winnie and Noah. She begged to be let off. It was not a rebellion, more like a nervous breakdown. Her parents relented, and persuaded the local schoolteacher to give her private tuition; but she was not victorious, she was sorry, and spent overlong hours studying school texts and exhausted elderly Miss Shelford with her sprint through the French irregular verbs and the length of her essays.

Further differences, difficulties too, came to light round about the age of puberty – Phil's almost coincided with her older siblings' and with her precocious younger ones'. She did not giggle about it, she did not refer to it, nor would she answer questions on that subject. She seemed to be ashamed. She turned against swimming with the opposite sex, spotty boys in particular. She had always liked to swim alone – no splashing, never horseplay. Now she swam at anti-social hours, often at dawn. And if she was persuaded to join in with the family, she would hide her figure as much as possible and never change out of her bathing-dress, towel notwithstanding, in public.

Yet she was loved in a special way, she was the family pet. Her elfin manners charmed. Her quietness was valued. Her scholarly achievements

99

did not deteriorate into competitiveness. She was apt to know more than her siblings being educated at the Cornish Academy, and her knowledge extended into unacademic areas, palmistry, for example, and the exercise of tact and grace.

The misfortunes of her three older siblings hit her hard. They were the first real sorrows for all the children of Castle Scar – and for their mother: their father had survived the 1914 war with no illusions to bless himself with. Phil had been close to Magda in one way, to Winnie in another, and to Noah in a third, before they had chosen to walk on paths more perilous than the one in the rock-face of the scar.

Magda's infatuation with Hitler was incomprehensible, almost everyone said so. But Phil had read of passion, its waywardness, and historical errors. The force of Magda's psyche would have been pent up by her religious faith and upbringing, she suggested, and released by exposure to a form of naked power, power being one of the immemorial aphrodisiacs. Magda had felt compelled to do as Hitler's soldiers had done at the rally. Phil sympathised with her. She aired not her reservations but her appreciation of Magda's generosity, followed by a sort of penance, her marriage to the father of her child, loss of her nationality, and a life of rootlessness and uncertainty stretching ahead.

Winnie also had done the decent thing in Phil's opinion, she had brought Peter into the world. Although the alternative was unthinkable, it could be arranged: the children of Castle Scar, rustic as they were, had heard tell of the wicked ways of the wider world.

Phil mourned Noah, and was sure he had meant well, sitting on that bomb; but she did allow herself to wonder how he could have been so obstinate as not to be swayed by the mounting evidence of the inhumanity of the Bolsheviks.

Phil was not a simpleton, far from it, her piety and her determination to look on the bright side cast a pale purifying glow over the whole family and its activities.

In her twenties she was filling out her elfin figure. She was developing in all ways, including a sudden fancy to sample the low-class romances that Adeline read and to deign to listen to mushy tunes on the wireless. She confessed to Father O'Malley that she had sinned by wondering if she would ever be pretty, would she be pretty enough? He said she had a good chance of finding love and happiness.

But she did not find anything like it. She met no male strangers. If she saw one, for instance on the beach, she swam out to sea or climbed up the path. She shopped with her mother, she went with her father to nursery gardens and vintners. She was taken to the cinema by a brother or a sister. She could talk freely to Jones for as long as he would let her. And time passed, and she spent more and more of it alone in the chapel.

One day she opened the front door in response to imperious knocking. A youngish man stood there. He said he had brought cases of wine for

Lord Penzoote. She indicated that he could bring them into the Castle – actually such deliveries were taken in at the tradesmen's entrance, but the man was too confident and authoritative to be redirected. He called out to a second man waiting by a blue van.

'In here, Joe!'

Joe began to load a trolley with wooden cases. His boss stepped over the threshold, shot out a hand for Phil to shake, and introduced himself.

'I'm Nigel Wallace-East. How do you do? You must be the daughter of the house.'

She whispered in reply to his loud address: 'I'm Phillis Hope.'

'How do?' he said, and then: 'You've got a mighty fine location, that's a fact. Would you be nice enough to show me your view?'

'All right,' she said.

He strode into the sitting-room and across to the great window at the far end.

'Marvellous!' he exclaimed in an unarguable tone. He turned back to her and said: 'Is that a chapel I passed?'

She said it was.

'Goodness me! Keeps you on the straight and narrow, doesn't it?'

She did not answer.

'Are your people around?'

'My mother's shopping and my father's in the garden.'

'Give them my respects. Do you get out much, Phillis?'

'What do you mean?'

'Out to hops, or the flicks?'

She shook her head.

'What about an outing? Would you like to shake a leg?'

She could not help laughing, because he embarrassed her, he was so cheeky and ridiculous.

In the hall he shouted at Joe: 'All done?'

He shook her limp chill hand and said: 'I'll give you a tinkle and check that you're up for a spot of fun. Cheerio!' And he was driven away by Joe in the blue van.

For uncertain reasons Phillis only told her father that his wine had arrived.

Nothing happened – again she was not sure whether she was relieved or disappointed. A second thought was that he was absolutely awful and a third that he was quite amusing. Then he rang her up. The month was May, it was a warm afternoon, Phillis was on her own in Castle Scar, the others were elsewhere, and she answered the telephone.

'Is that Phillis?' he demanded.

'Who are you?' she asked

'Nigel – I was thinking of a swim – could we swim down in your bay?'

'I don't swim.'

'I'll teach you.'

'No.'

'Well, I could swim, couldn't I?'

'All right.'

'Okay – ta-ta!'

His car was small, red, open and noisy. She was waiting for him by the gravel circle where cars were parked – the last thing she wanted was to have to introduce him to her family – and led him by the circuitous public right of way to the path at the top of the scar. She meant not to get involved in his swimming, but he objected.

'You could come down with me,' he said in a reproachful tone of voice.

She did so. He had a paper bag containing a swimsuit and towel. On the beach he removed his tweed jacket, then his waistcoat.

'Hold up my towel, will you?'

It was more an order than a question. She held it with her face averted. He changed into a one-piece red swimsuit with a union jack printed on the chest area, and ran into the sea. He had hairy thin muscular legs, and he ran in an ugly way and swam side-stroke, which the Hope children despised. When he emerged dripping and she was holding out his towel, he inquired, 'Like a nice wet hug?' and laughed when she shook her head. He dressed and they climbed back up the path. Her parents and Adeline were having tea on the terrace.

Phil was mortified. She blushed, she felt she was on fire. She had been praying not to have to introduce Nigel to anyone, she was ashamed of him, and dreaded jumps to conclusions. He introduced himself. He did that wrong, too. He was familiar with her father and mother, and said to Addie: 'You'll be the other sister.' Was he comparing Addie and Phil to the Ugly Sisters in *Cinderella*?

Mary Penzoote offered him tea. Phil was furious with her. Nigel addressed her father impertinently.

'You enjoying your wine, Lord Penzoote?' he asked.

Edward was non-plussed.

'I work at Murray and Murray,' Nigel said, referring to the Penzootes' wine merchants. 'I had a couple of cases delivered to you the other day. Your pretty daughter showed me round the place.'

'Oh yes,' Edward acknowledged vaguely.

The cup of tea was carried out of the house by Addie and served to Nigel.

'Thank you kindly,' he said. And he began to talk to Edward about wines.

Phil escaped indoors. Addie followed her, giggling and saying: 'Look at his clothes!' Nigel wore a loud check tweed suit, three piece, with silver fob linking the waistcoat pockets, and a pink carnation in his buttonhole: Phil had been too tense to notice. Addie made matters worse. 'And he's so ugly,' she said. Phil peeped through the French window at his bulbous eyes, shark-like mouth and receding chin.

She returned to the terrace and interrupted his monologue by saying: 'I'll take you to your car.'

She was more embarrassed by the way he said 'Au revoir' to her parents. But Addie laughed at him for telling her, 'I'll be seeing you again,' and Phil felt sorry for his cheekiness and ignorance. When he asked if she would fancy a matinee at the cinema on the next Saturday afternoon, she said, 'Well...'

That time at the cinema he insisted on holding

her unresponsive hand. The next time she let him put an arm round her shoulders and nuzzle the side of her head. After the third film he took her to a tea-room where they danced, and he kissed her cold lips goodbye when he had driven her back to Castle Scar.

She was amazed by herself and not pleased with him. She was not attracted, she was behaving out of character and badly. He put her teeth on edge, jarred upon and bored her. On the other hand he was a novelty and she had nothing to do. Such materialistic realities would not have moved her fastidious person to dally with Nigel Wallace-East. Pity was her motive. For all his faults she was sorry. His manners were bravado: she had only not to smile at him, and he would say, 'Have I done wrong again? Have I blown it again?' He was snobbish, on the make, aimed preposterously high, counted his chickens while he smashed his eggs: the disappointments in store for him brought tears to her eyes. She felt protective, bound to protect him, and failed to count the costs.

He lived with his parents and a sister in a terrace house in Trepenison. His father worked on the railways, his mother had been Miss East, his sister was a shopgirl. They were obviously on their best behaviour when Phil came to tea. Nigel's job at Murray and Murray was precarious: he was in charge of deliveries and seemed to be in hot water regularly. He paid for their cinema tickets with very small change he kept in a purse, and spread the expense of their outings over six weeks.

She meant to say goodbye and good riddance. Addie warned Rudy that Nigel was a dead loss, and Rudy, after meeting him, called him 'Nigel the nightmare'. Phil was bracing herself to give him his marching orders when he turned up one afternoon in July, unannounced, in an agitated state, and with his swimming gear in the same crumpled paper bag.

Displeasure took precedence over pity. She said she was busy, but would let him have a quick swim – no more. He proposed marriage on the path to the beach. She told him not to be silly, and, still more crisply, because he covered his eyes with his hands in a gesture of despair, not to fall down the scar. They sat on the sand while he argued the point. He needed her badly, he might be losing his job, he wanted to start all over again, and she was 'a bit of all right' and would inspire him to work hard and make good money.

'I don't love you, I never will,' she tried to din into him, but he did not understand her language any more than she was swayed by his selfish ramblings.

At length she said: 'Well, do you want to swim or don't you?'

The rigmarole with the towel was repeated and he swam on his side. She would have left him to dry himself and dress if the beach had been empty, but there were family parties in the vicinity who might object to his nudity. She therefore again held the towel for him until he called her name in an odd voice. She looked over the edge of the towel, saw he had no clothes on, was fiddling with himself, and heard him say between gasps: 'I'm proving I could be a good husband for you.' She screamed. He had the grace to turn his back and pull on a pair of pants. She threw the towel at him and clambered up the path, ran indoors and locked herself in the lavatory on the attic floor of the Castle, where she and her siblings slept. Her parents with Addie, Rudy, Zac and Viv were all out, they had gone to a tennis party with neighbours. She prayed that Nigel would not search for her and do her bodily harm. She prayed doubtfully to be left alone. At last she heard the sound of the engine of his car, revving up and receding into the distance. She began to cry.

Her hysterical crying was prolonged. After several days of it, Mary called in Dr Hopkinson. But Phil's illnesses were not curable by an aspirin or a bottle of tonic. She was beset by disgust. Nigel's sex act for her benefit was the most counterproductive of his version of sweet nothings. He not only repelled her once and for ever, he did it so thoroughly that she told Addie she could never face love made to her by any man. She swore she would not marry. She was frightened, her secondary complaint was fear.

She had not been far wrong in the lavatory. She was bombarded by letters from Nigel, threatening, whimpering, badly written and misspelt. She read a few and was still more afraid. His begging was combined with details of how he intended to torture her if she did not fall

108

into his arms – or even if she did, for he wished to punish her for rejecting his proposal. He played the class card – she was too rich and arrogant to appreciate the love of a poor man. He invoked her religion – she was a hypocrite to go to her foreign church, she was a false Christian with her chapel and her cruelty. He said he had written to Father O'Malley, he did write to Edward Penzoote and separately to Mary, and he waylaid Addie in the High Street at Trepenison and called her another bitch and a so-and-so.

Phil was afflicted with cowardice, panic, phobias. She neither ate nor slept properly, and became a shadow of that shadow which had been herself. She was confined to her bedroom, locked in, only emerging to collect small quantities of food and briefly to pray in the chapel. She refused ministrations offered by her mother, did not respond to her father's knocking on her bedroom door, and told her siblings to go away.

Edward obtained a legal injunction, which forbade Nigel to harass Phillis, but poison pen communications referring to no one in particular were found on the beach and in the grounds of the Castle. A posse of her three brothers sought Nigel in his house, but his parents and his sister Gladys blocked the door, said he was out, and that he was considering breach of promise litigation. The brothers then went to Murray and Murray's premises, where they were told that Nigel was no longer in the firm's employment.

Phil was not grateful for their efforts to spare

her. The most complicating factor of her breakdown was that her terror of Nigel was mixed up with sympathy for him and her responsibility for driving him at least half-mad. Her family lost patience with her moans about poor Nigel and everything being her fault. The siblings began to urge her to pull herself together.

The solution of the problem was unexpected. According to the local newspapers Nigel Wallace-East was engaged to marry Mary-Ann Maister. The Maisters lived farther along the Cornish coast in the westward direction. They had recently bought an estate called Tremallivan. They were a Canadian family, and Mary-Ann was their only child.

Phil recovered gradually, over many months, and rejoined the family for meals and services in the chapel. Although Winnie, behind her back, compared her to a bird with a broken wing, and Viv said she was one of the walking wounded, she showed tentative signs of becoming more positive and even decisive. One winter evening in the dining-room, after Edward and Mary had absented themselves to listen to news on the wireless, the Band of Hope discussed its aims as the candles burned low and the bottles of wine circulated. Phil intervened, which was unusual.

'You all want to change the world,' she said, 'but I don't.'

Surprised faces turned to look at her – she had never been known to disagree with anybody, except Nigel Wallace-East.

'I hate change,' she continued. 'I'd never change

anything by force. Evolution's unstoppable, I suppose, but revolution's an awful mistake. Revolt's different, it's brave to revolt against injustice. Please ... Animals don't make revolutions, they behave better than we do. Why did Magda side with those Nazis? Why was Noah all for those Bolsheviks? It beats me! Hitler's making an army, and armies are for war, and wars are fought for change – oh dear! I haven't lived much, not as much as you all have, but I've read a lot. I must have read more than Magda and Noah, because I knew Hitler was ghastly when she didn't, and guessed communism was more so from every point of view. Women's weakness is to get personal, and I shouldn't but I will – Nigel tried to change our friendship and I'll never be the same – no, no, I'm not angling for sympathy! No, I'm a cautionary tale. I wish the Band of Hope wouldn't try to invent a new heaven and earth. Your goals are in Erehwon, they are, and Erehwon's nowhere spelt backwards. Please let us all be! Please don't risk your own lives and the peace of mind of everybody else by leading us over the edge of our world!'

The day after Phil's outburst Edward spoke to Jones in the garden.

'Phil's getting better,' he said.

'I'm glad to hear that.'

'She told off the others yesterday evening.'

'Oh ah?'

'She told them to stop pushing their new-fangled schemes.'

'Did she now?'

'She spoke up against change.'

'What sort of change would that be?'

'Any sort, so far as I can gather.'

'Trouble is, we're temporary – we're not where we are for long.'

'She must be too young to have thought of that.'

'I expect she is, sir.'

RUDOLPH

Rudy, the fifth of the eight children of Edward and Mary Penzoote, was always fat. His mother was painfully aware of the greed of his infancy; and when he had teeth, he did not chew with them, he somehow assimilated unusually large quantities of food.

He developed the features that go with his type of digestion, the small nose in the large round face. He waddled, too, and his nature was lazy, good-humoured but averse to physical exertion. At the same time his brain worked overtime. It had its own form of the ability to assimilate: it seemed to suck in and store knowledge. He shone at exams at school and won a scholarship to university.

The Hope children in their pre-pubic state were not sentimental. They fell in love with ideas rather than with people. They thought of the animal kingdom in terms of protein.

Their coming of age was not marked by the boys' discovery that in a sexual sense they were men, or the girls' realisation that they could make a baby, but by the assumption and presumption that they knew how to improve the lot of the human race. They wanted to do good for their fellows, for the flesh and blood of whom they actually cared nothing; and they were too clever to bother their heads with common sense. Their puberty, their testosterone, imbued each of them in turn with unshakeable confidence that they were born to right the wrongs of the world.

For Magda it had been the recognition of the power of power; for Winnie, promiscuity convinced her that women were worth more alimony than she had received; for Noah, the saviour was Karl Marx, the grand panjandrum of the unintended consequence; and for Phil, the nihilism of a suspension of nearly all signs of life. Rudy branched out into Africa. He did so in a literary manner to begin with. He read books about Africa, romances set in Africa, learned studies of African history, missionaries' diaries, scientists' findings, geographers' reports. He then wrote his doctoral thesis on a subject that had escaped the notice of European scholarship, *The Culture of Central Africa.* On reaching the time of life at which his siblings seemed to enter into their exploratory phases, he resolved to go to the dark continent.

His aims were mixed, even confused. He wanted to check that the colonial authorities were governing the people better than they could govern themselves: it would save trouble to support colonialism. He would like to offer practical assistance if needed to the more primitive tribes, educational encouragement, maybe, nothing agricultural. He was quite keen to study the

116

races, the wildlife, the traditional wisdom of a civilisation originating from a primeval slime older than ours in the Palaearctic region. And he could do with a holiday.

He was mocked. His brothers and sisters were against his going. They reminded him that the African character was not exclusively gentle and receptive, it was also aggressive and belligerent. He was so plump that he would be of great interest to the cannibals still lurking in the African jungle. If he was thinking of missionary work, and preaching the Christian religion, he should beware of the ability of pagans to incorporate their misunderstandings of the Holy Bible into their orgiastic rites: the word 'blood' could serve the interests of lust as well as promoting piety.

Rudy was undeterred. He in his turn mocked the picture of himself in Africa that they seemed to be drawing, in his birthday suit, prancing round a camp fire that was boiling somebody in a big pot for supper. He would not stray into regions where white men had never set foot, he had his itinerary at his fingertips, and he would be even more inoffensive in Africa than he was in Cornwall. He believed he might unearth in that possible cradle of our race the panacea for all the ills of the old world – and perhaps the new world, too – for which the Band of Hope was searching with might and main.

Admittedly, he was short of practical experience of African weather, transportation and living conditions; but he was prepared for setbacks and discomfort. His plan was to take ship from

Tilbury to Port Abeegee on the western coast, in the Ivory Coast, to be precise, and travel by any means available due east towards Lake Chad. His luggage would be a haversack and sleeping bag. The haversack would contain a minimum of spare clothing, medicines, glucose tablets, beads for presents, maps and a New Testament. He was forced by the family to parade in full African gear and duly obliged. He wore boots, cotton socks, reaching to his knees, khaki shorts and vest, cotton jacket with multiple pockets, belt with holster for pistol and hunting knife in sheath, sun-glasses, souwester, solar topee fixed to the top of his haversack and water bottle dangling below.

'What about food?' he was asked.

'I'll procure it as I go along,' he replied.

'Shoot it with your pistol,' they asked; 'or hack it to death with your knife?'

'Buy it,' he said after the laughter had subsided.

'Where will you keep your money?'

He showed them. Golden sovereigns were secured on the inner surface of the headband of his topee, and in secret compartments in the heels of his boots.

'What or who will you shoot with your pistol?' they asked, and reminded him that he had no 'eye' for games.

He made everyone laugh louder by saying: 'In the last resort I'll shoot myself.'

He left Castle Scar in a grey suit and with suitcases – the suit would be needed on the voyage, especially for dinner at the Captain's table. His father wished him luck, his mother called on God to protect him, his siblings sped him on his way with jokes.

Six weeks later a postcard franked with Ivory Coast stamps, but showing a picture of the vessel in which Rudolph had shipped to Africa, was delivered to 'All at Castle Scar'. He wrote: 'Arrived at Abeegee. Weather boiling hot. Feels funny being a paleface here. Setting off tomorrow by train into interior. You won't hear from me for a bit. Love R.'

It caused annoyance. Rudy had not bothered to write more fully, not spent money on a card superior to a snapshot of *The Merchantman of Tilbury*, not supplied any information that would be useful in an emergency – he had been neglectful as well as lazy. That he had taken the trouble to get himself to Africa, and probably meet his end there, was a surprise and not a pleasant one. The consensus was that he was a sleepy old pussycat who had padded into the land of lions.

However, he slowly made hearts fonder in the home of the Hopes. Rudy stayed away for the expected six weeks; and not long afterwards he was gone for six months. A year after his departure, Edward Penzoote was prevailed upon by Mary to address an inquiry to the Colonial Office in Whitehall. It drew a blank. The representatives of the British government in the Ivory Coast and the countries leading to and surrounding Lake Chad were also unable to help. No one had ever met, seen or heard of an Englishman

119

in a solar topee bent on solitary travel through areas fraught with a variety of perils.

The fate of Noah was now invoked by the mother of Rudy, and Magdalen's destiny was thrown into her argument: was she to lose one dear child, mislay another, and never again to set eyes on a third? She begged God or someone else to do something about rescuing her Rudy or his earthly remains. After a scrap of sibling humour to the effect that Rudy would be difficult to find in Africa although he could hardly be compared to a needle, the task fell to Addie – in fact she had volunteered for it months before – and brother Zac offered to accompany her.

Their travel was more like travail. Their voyage on *The Merchantman of Tilbury* was sentimental, also nearly the death of them – the ship was damaged in an Atlantic storm. In Africa they were immediately struck down, if not quite down and out, by the equatorial climate, their lack of Rudy's linguistic skills, the hungry insects, and the indigestible food. They sweated profusely for days and nights in a train, ached all over after camel rides in an easterly direction, froze at night under the stars, and then had thirty-six hours in a bus that stopped more than it started. They were eventually deposited in an oasis village said to be not far from Lake Chad. No news of Rudy was obtainable, they had no idea of where to go next, they could not communicate properly with anyone, no transport in any direction was on offer, let alone a guide, and they were based in a lodging house where they ate disgusting food and slept in a crowded unisex yard with crude lavatorial amenities.

One day traders arrived with fresh fruits and vegetables for sale. While Addie and Zac were buying stuff, a sinister figure, hawk-nosed and hairy, swathed in colourful shawls, spoke to them. He said with an upper class accent, 'Good morning, Madam, good morning, Sir – not bad weather today.' They guessed, they were sure he had been taught English by their brother. He then said, 'Rudy?' and pointed interrogatively towards the hills. Addie found it hard to believe that he was offering to take them to where Rudy was, Zac suspected that they would be eaten as Rudy might have been. They nonetheless replied in unison, 'Yes, yes,' and followed him.

Their next journey was by mule, uphill, in a caravan of horticultural tribesmen, it seemed, whose leader repeated his single English phrase – 'Good morning, not bad weather' – even at night while freezing winds blew. But he treated his 'Madam' and 'Sir' with deference, and fed them well – fed them up maybe – on food that was yet another mystery, tender meat and luscious berries.

At last, passing through a narrow defile at the top of a mountain, they saw a deep valley below, bathed in sunshine, vividly green, watered by streams and pools, and receding into a misty distance. They were dazzled, stunned. Smoke rose from a large village or a small township. Their guide was pointing and calling out, 'Burraka!' He laughed, Addie and Zac laughed, urged their

121

mules to hurry unsuccessfully, and in due course were reunited with their brother.

He said he was safe, safe and well, but he was changed almost beyond recognition. He had been an overweight young man, he was as near as nothing obese. He had long hair and wore Burrakan attire, a short dressing gown of coloured cloth. He was psychologically altered, too. He asked for news of the family, but lost interest in accounts of Phil's craze for conservation and Viv's academic trophies. He asked Addie to give his love to their parents, speaking listlessly but perhaps indicating without delay that he had no intention of being taken home by anybody.

Addie and Zac had arrived in the middle of day one of their sojourn in Burraka: 'in time for lunch', as Rudy put it. They were immediately served with pottery beakers of saha, a fruity beverage, by almost naked sweetly smiling youths and maidens. Over a meal of tasty nuggets of unidentified food, the siblings swapped their traveller's tales. Rudy had stumbled into Burraka by accident. He had been welcomed because he was fat – he explained that Burrakans were uniformly slender, a fat man therefore looked to them like a god, another Buddha. A king or some unseen person or some governmental committee had invited him to stay in the palace – there was room in it for his sister and brother. In answer to questions of the sociological type, he said that food was plenteous, farmers produced it in the northern region, the valley was fertile, pure water flowed from snowy mountains into its pools and on to southern lowlands, and peace and joy seemed in effect to rule Burraka.

Those beakers were filled and refilled with saha. A celebratory mood, a mood of good humour and light-heartedness took over. The siblings had a laugh over the Burrakan lingo with its stuttering and clicks: Zac and Addie marvelled at Rudy's ability to pronounce it.

Was he happy in his hideaway, Addie asked.

Absolutely!

Would he, could he, escape from Burraka, and could they, Zac wondered idly.

Of course!

The part of the palace occupied by the three members of the Band of Hope was a bungalow of sorts, a roof, a wooden floor, divided by curtains of brightly coloured material into 'rooms'. The roof covered an extended verandah, greenery surrounded the building, huge green leaves intruded into the 'rooms', and strange animals and birds moved in the vicinity and emitted growls and cries, squawks, honks and songs, unlike anything heard in Cornwall. The hygienic arrangements were not bad, a cold water shower was curtained off, and there was a gully with water running through and a plank of wood across it.

The two travellers were tired out and rested in their rooms after the meal that Rudy called luncheon. Both slept for hours, more soundly than they had since leaving Castle Scar, and into the dawn of the next day. The three siblings breakfasted together, again with saha, and Addie and Zac drowsed for more hours on the verandah.

123

After dinner that evening Rudy suggested a swim, but warned that he himself swam in the nude and no spare swimsuits were available. The usual crowd of Burrakan boys and girls were already escorting them towards the pool, while Zac said he had never fancied a skinny dip in public, and Addie said, 'No, thanks!' The dusk was illuminated by the African moon. The water in the pool was like a black mirror, reflecting moonbeams, and overhung by the branches of flowering trees. Strong scents mingled with the cries and laughter of the young people as they dropped their apologies for clothing and leapt and submerged themselves in the water. Rudy followed suit and jumped in with a tremendous splash. He was surrounded, the girls were all round him, the boys were stirring up the activity, and the cries were more like moans and grunts. At a certain moment Addie glanced at Zac and vice versa. They had seen or thought they had seen an improper act in progress, and when they ventured to look again at the scene in the water they saw Rudy was gasping for breath, he was being applauded, other orgiastic things were happening, and they had witnessed a sexual free-for-all.

Addie was determined to scold Rudolph for behaviour offensive from both secular and religious points of view, and Zac said he was ready to support her. They marched away and up to the palace, intending to give Rudy a piece of their minds when he rejoined them. But they drank another beaker or two of saha, and an unwonted tolerance blurred the outlines of Addie's puritanical conscience, and Zac saw the funny side of the situation.

The three siblings lolled on cushions on the verandah, in the moonglow, and at last without the young courtiers, who had retreated into the night.

'Rudy,' Addie began, 'what is this stuff we've been drinking?'

'The national drink of Burraka, the common denomination of the nation, peculiar to this valley and unknown elsewhere, a mystery, a secret, and nectar that solves all problems – is that enough of an answer to your question?'

'No.'

Rudy sighed and laughed and said: 'I only know it must be made of fruits and herbs. But...'

'It's intoxicating, isn't it?'

'It has psychological effects, and some physical ones too – yes, it's intoxicating.'

'Zac and I feel we've been drugged ever since we came here.'

'Not drugged, modified – saha's a saving grace.'

'What are you talking about, Rudy?'

'Saha has modified you, Addie – you'll find out soon – and Zac, you'll benefit from a course of modification – it'll strike a balance between your brain and your body.'

Zac giggled and said: 'It's transformed you into twice the man you were, Rudy, that's clear enough.'

They all laughed, then Addie said, 'Be serious, Rudy,' although in a less serious tone of voice than she intended.

'I was trying to be, but you interrupted me. Saha's more than just a slightly alcoholic drink with a nice taste. In my considered view, it's the elixir we've all been seeking since we were evicted from the Garden of Eden. As a member of the Band of Hope, I regard it differently, I see it as salvation.'

'Hell's bells!' Zac exclaimed.

Addie said: 'You can't pretend that saha's the very thing you came to find in Africa – it's not a messiah!'

'I do, it is – no, listen! Burraka's a miracle. In a continent almost created from blood and tears, which militates sooner or later against human contentment, it's a pleasure ground, a society that functions, a natural phenomenon locked in by unscalable mountains, self-sufficient, green and beautiful. How do you think the people of this happy land manage not to be ambitious, restless, curious, competitive, envious, warlike? How do they cure the original sinfulness of our race? Answer in two syllables, saha. Compare Burraka with Cornwall, with England, with the rest of the world, and Burrakans with our contemporaries at the end of their tethers, the sick in body and soul, the victimisers and the victims, the wicked politicians, the criminals! We, our Band of Hope, make it an article of faith that our country, England, is in decline, at a dead end, poised on the very edge of *finito*. The modern world is an impossible place, no one can live in the worst versions of it satisfactorily. Well, what I've found in Africa is a remedy, a panacea, another chance. I foresee a future of saha, or, if you like to call a spade a bloody shovel, drugs. Medicine will make advances, new drugs will be available, harsh reality will be kept at bay, children and robots will fight our wars, nobody will need to know anything horrid. Saha would make the best of the worst conditions men can contrive. If the composition of saha could be discovered, it should be administered forcibly to the masses, for example by means of the water supply. That's my serious contribution to discussions we've always had – saha would knock some of the stuffing out of life, out of man's aspirations, but it would improve its quality, kill pain, promote friendship and love.'

Zac's comment on this speech was, 'Whew!'

Laughter greeted his witty sally.

Addie said: 'Are you suggesting we're all going to be drugged from the cradle to the grave?'

'I'm betting we will be – and hoping saha will do the trick.'

After a pause for cogitation, Zac spoke.

'What about the increase in populations? If events in the pool this evening are anything to go by, and saha's to blame for these events – excesses, I might say – birthrates would be much higher and the world would be still more overcrowded. What about that?'

'Drugs can kill as well as cure. Saha would make life as bearable as it's surely meant to be.'

'And religion, Rudy?'

'That's for another evening. Have some more saha. All will be well, Addie.'

127

'You were always such an optimist,' she retorted.

They were tired – naturally or because of their intake of soporific essences. They went to bed. They went nowhere else. They really got nowhere, and the days passed between the heaven of the limbo-land of Burraka and the hell of postponed inquiries and decisions. They ate too much, put on weight, drank too much, forgot their absent family, and drifted separately through the timeless freedom of the eternal summer of nowhere. Old principles and values surfaced briefly on occasions. Addie said with untypical giggles that she was appalled by the prospect of Great Britain zonked out on drugs. Zac said he had heard of the end of civilisations that had chosen the path of insensibility, and looked forward to such a fate overtaking poor old England. Addie and Zac should have been more dismayed than they were to discover that Burrakans were so jolly thanks to another property of saha: unwelcome intruders, old and ill folk, and wrongdoers were given more than was good for them and died of delight. They turned blind eyes to illiberal laws and a hierarchical social structure – hedonism was more fun than finding fault. The journey back to where hair shirts were worn in foul weather was postponed.

One evening Addie refused the offer of saha. Her brothers reproached her, called her a spoilsport, and the little brown playmates cajoled her in sign language, with patting and stroking her extremities and kissing her toes. She would not relent. Rudy and Zac went for their usual swim in the pool, and, later, tried to tot up the number of mixed-race babies they must have added to the Burrakan genetic stock. Addie announced that she at any rate was going home.

She wrote out a telegram and entrusted the piece of paper to the hawk-nosed market gardener, who was instructed by Rudy to give it to the next leader of a caravan bound for cities equipped with telephonic apparatus. Golden sovereigns were wrapped in the paper, money to pay for the transmission of the message and to reward the bearer.

Strange to relate, many weeks later the telegram reached Castle Scar.

Jones was informed in due course.

'They're due back in a week or two, all three of them,' Edward said.

'That's a good job,' Jones commented.

'There's a saying, "always something new out of Africa".'

'Oh ah?'

'It doesn't say if the new thing's good or bad.'

'Time'll tell.'

'Quite so!'

ADELINE

Addie did not really deserve her surname. She seemed to have been born without hope. She was a prim child, a stand-offish girl, an awkward young woman, and her academic success did not make her more amenable or charming. She grew to be tall, like Magda, but lacked Magda's pretty face. She was gawky and pigeon-toed – and nothing like Winnie. She had a protuberant forehead and a long nose that was apt to go red at the tip after she had eaten and in cold weather. She suffered from chilblains on her large hands and feet in winter, and in summer from hay fever. She was not a smiler, but could laugh rather loud and occasionally giggle. Her intelligence informed her early on that she was plain, and, since she was sensitive and had a romantic temperament, she felt she had nothing much to smile at.

Being one of eight cut both ways for Addie. Her brothers were not the opposite sex in a meaningful sense; on the other hand they refrained from judging her by her looks. Her brain did not single her out from her siblings, who were also brainy, but she won admiration from the family who could appreciate her leadership qualities – she was allowed to exercise her streak of bossiness. Luckily she was so preoccupied by her brothers and sisters and the scope of their discussions at Castle Scar that she never tried too hard to catch a man.

Her attitudes to the members of her family describe her mentality. She honoured her father because she was in awe of his worldly wisdom and cynicism. She took her mother for granted, but appreciated her usefulness and reliability.

She was scornful of Magda's infatuation with Adolf Hitler. Magda's yearning for power was muddled: what power would she acquire by sleeping with Hitler or conceiving his child, and what did she think she could have done with the power she never acquired? Magda had misunderstood the aims of the Band of Hope, and received her desserts in the form of the 'waxwork'.

Winnie's wild life in London was enviable, but the fatherhood of her child was a farce. Addie agreed with Winnie that the spoils of matrimony should be divided at least more equally than they were, but she took no interest in the subject, she did not expect to marry.

Noah and Addie were not close. Noah was not close with anyone. He lived for fish, which swallowed his hooked flies and died for him. He was another muddle – they were all muddlers in Addie's private opinion. Noah laid down his life – or, in fact, sat down – for Lenin and Stalin, men whose names were aliases, who were shams and tin gods.

Phil was a contradiction of hope. If she had not been a feeble person, Addie would have crushed her underfoot. For Phil had had the chance that Addie would have given most of her accomplishments for, and had spurned it. Admittedly, Nigel Wallace-East could be called a catastrophe rather than a chance, but where he had trod other men might have followed – Phil was a virgin and a spinster by choice, believe it or not.

Rudy's susceptibility to the magnet of Africa unsettled Addie. She listened to his talk of gold and diamonds, striking it rich, savage biology, the gigantic scale of the continent and everything in it, also of historic blood-letting and esoteric torture, and associated the law of the African jungle with sex. She referred to Rudy's quest in objective terms – could be of scientific interest; but, physiologically, it put a sharper edge on her sexual hunger.

Rudy departed – Addie waved goodbye with envy. Then his prolonged silence, the cause of concern to others, fuelled the fires of her imagination. She thought of him in the arms of black girls, she thought of herself in the arms of black boys. And her psyche became a battleground. She was a devout Catholic and kept the rules of her church. Her god was the man in her life. She believed that she owed her grey cells to Him, and that He expected her not to complain of not having been endowed with sex appeal as well. The Christian teaching was not to be greedy – greed was one of the cardinal

135

sins. She could cope so long as she was not led into temptation, not reminded of flesh and the sins thereof, for instance by Magda, Winnie, Phil and now Rudy; but deliverance from evil was not quickly forthcoming in answer to her prayers.

The consensus in the family, as Rudy's absence grew sinister, was that a rescue operation should be mounted. Addie volunteered, Zac ditto, and, after one of those odysseys that cry out to be cut short in the telling, they achieved their object.

Burraka was sensuously warm and fruitful. Life there was untrammelled by rules and regulations, and seemed to be out of reach of the wrath of God. Rudy was changed for the better and fatter. And a sort of tonic wine, surely organic, much more beneficial than British beer and spirits, and with no noticeably harmful side-effects, was an integral part of the staple diet and on offer day and night.

In addition, swimming in a pool of clean water at an agreeable temperature was the done thing. Addie watched Rudy being undressed and assisted into the pool by stark naked and lovely and laughing teenagers of both sexes, and rubbed her eyes and ground her teeth. When she and one brother saw their other brother engaging in an undoubted if unspeakable act of group-sex in the water, she was shocked and blushed to the very roots of her hair. She walked away, she dragged Zac away. She told Zac that Burraka had robbed Rudy of his status as an English gentleman. She said saha spelt goodbye to modesty and reserve.

Back in the palace she drank some more of it to steady her nerves, and consequently was not so down on Rudy as she had meant to be. The three of them giggled together whenever they spoke of 'swimming'. A few days later both brothers rejoined Addie in the palace, their hair wet and smug expressions on their faces. Soon, Rudy and Zac's dip after dinner became an almost regular entertainment, and Addie had to increase her intake of saha. It numbed her conscience. Late one evening, when her siblings happened to be befuddled and somnolent, she headed for the pool.

She was accompanied by a dozen or so accomplices. The night air was balmy, the moon silvered the surfaces of greenery, the heady scents attracted great moths that soared and settled on the trumpet-shaped flowers. The handmaidens twittered and giggled, stroked her and plucked at her clothing. Boys slid into the dark water reflecting the moon and beckoned her with white smiles and glistening eyes. She let her clothes drop, and stood on the brink of her destiny. Heavy-breasted and with hips made for bearing children, she held out her hands and fleshy arms to her attendants and allowed herself to be pulled into the pool.

She sank into a mixture of soft water and a cushion of the limbs of the little people of both sexes. They paddled her gently into deeper water, out of her depth in all senses, and tipped her on to her back, her side, her front, and in each position she was initiated without difficulty into the facilities of the female anatomy. Enjoyment banished care, pleasure took precedence over prudence. Water seemed to wash away sin. She was laughing too, she was no longer Adeline Hope, she was aquatic, a fish, an elegant jellyfish, a sponge. Girls were touching and tickling her while the boys would be boys, and the moon looked down unshocked, and the night-birds whooped and whistled in the outlandish mode of Burraka.

The game was played out, she reclothed herself, bade her brothers good night, and slept as never before, the sleep of fulfilment and readiness for a repeat performance. A transformation had occurred, sex was now reality for her, life without it was mere impatience. Night after night more of her bitter history was expunged in the pool, for she was desirous and desired.

But the clock ticked, and one day she told her brothers she was going home. They were blackmailed into accompanying her, they could not let her go alone. Their farewells to Burraka were regretful: they were all addicted to its loveliness and sex, and its saha, none of which they were allowed to take out of the country. Rudy ameliorated the sorrow of parting by promising to return as soon as possible, and never to forget his illegitimate offspring or their mothers and mothers-to-be. Zac was sorry to see the last of a land where nobody complained. Addie cried on the shoulders of a small regiment of her lovers.

They had withdrawal symptoms on the journey.

Addie was sickened by the more genuine African food. They were not in the mood for sight-seeing. They snapped at one another across half the continent. They resigned themselves to the voyage north in *The Merchantman of Tilbury*.

The moment they landed Addie made an excuse and took a taxi to Harley Street. She had sent another telegram to a gynaecologist, Dr Matthews. His diagnosis was not a surprise. The surprise was, the worst news was, that she was pregnant with triplets.

She broke the news at Castle Scar. Her parents showed how unusual they were. Her mother was sorry for her, her father's comment was, 'Not you, too!' Her siblings were more or less embarrassed. Nobody had ever had triplets in Edward's family or in Mary's – nobody had had twins. Nobody in Cornwall known to the Hopes or read about in their newspapers had had triplets. Triplets were somehow scandalous – science had not yet discovered how to give women litters, like sows.

The prurient curiosity was almost as bad for Addie as the public opinion that triplets were an offence. Would three babies at once bust her guts? Think of her labour – one baby was more than enough for most women! How were three to be breast-fed – she was thirty-three per cent short of the requisite equipment? The nappies, which were not throwaway in those days, were the subject of dirty jokes, and the costs of hot water, soap, clothes-pegs and the extra help Addie would need were counted. How was she to manage, people asked, and what would happen to her figure after it had been stretched to accommodate three large babies?

The next question was the worst. Who was the father? Rudy was called upon to account for the length of his stay in Africa, say where he had been, and why he had failed to keep an eye on his sister. Zac was asked similar questions. For Addie, their answers and her own threatened to shine a lurid light on lovely fun that looked much less funny in Cornwall.

Interrogations were conducted in front of parents as well as siblings. Rudy began by describing Burraka, the fact that it was an exception to most African rules, its superiority to materialism and militarism, and the good fortune of its people. Zac chimed in by saying he had learnt a lot sociologically in Burraka. Mary thought it sounded very nice, Edward looked for it in vain in the Encyclopaedia Britannica, and Viv, the scientist, expressed scepticism.

'Who runs the show?' he wanted to know.

Some man or some unseen bureaucracy, Rudy replied, an authority that lets the people be free, quite different from government in England.

'An invisible authority is a contradiction in terms.'

'Don't be a pedant, Viv!'

'Well, how does the economy work?'

'Ask me another! We were guests of the nation, it wasn't up to us to spy on our hosts and demand details of their GNP.'

'Well, then, how is discipline maintained?'

'In the last resort by means of capital punishment administered by excessive consumption of their national alcoholic refreshment called saha.'

Rudy's answer was deliberately provocative. A hackneyed argument ensued: Viv supported by Winnie were against the death penalty, Phil with her obsessive hatred of change was equally against killers and against killing them. Mary repeated her view that to cause death in cold blood was rather awful. Edward said the guvnor of Burraka sounded like a good egg.

Winnie asked: 'Do you have to drink yourself to death if you steal a melon?'

'Probably.'

'Did you say "probably"?'

'I don't know, I probably did.'

'Shame on you, Rudy! I pity those poor African people, and feel sure you were the guests of another monstrous dictator.'

'Wrong, Winnie, wrong again! Not all Africans are poor, and Burrakans are as happy as our island race is sad. They have good food, good weather, no crime, almost no immigration, and saha, the most delicious of drinks, is the cure for all the ailments of the human condition. The people who are entitled to drink it live in heaven compared with the relative hell of our modern so-called "new Jerusalem".'

When the red herrings had been chased out of sight and out of mind, Phil asked Rudy: 'Why were you allowed to stay in Burraka? Why weren't you an immigrant?'

Rudy exchanged glances with Addie and Zac,

then replied: 'They thought we were good for their country.'

Viv re-entered the fray.

'Good in what sense? Were you trying to convert pagans to Roman Catholicism?'

'Burrakans have no formal religion, that's why they don't wage war.'

'If you weren't missionairies, what were you doing?'

'Improving the stock of the natives, creating new blood.'

'Come again!'

'Burrakans don't want to be inbred.'

'Were you introducing our genes into an African tribe?'

'We did what the Burrakans do, and what comes naturally. Our generation of our family is pretty much of a dead loss in that respect, eight of us in our lusty youth have so far produced only Winnie's Peter and Magda's teutonic issue.'

'Well,' Viv said, 'Addie's making a generous contribution in that line.'

The Penzootes happened not to be present when the debate was taking so personal a turn.

Winnie now put her oar in.

'I know I shouldn't be asking you this question, Addie, because I myself have had a spot of bother about answering it, but can you tell me who is the father of your triplets?'

'Not exactly,' Addie replied.

'Was it a native?'

Zac queried defensively: 'A native of Burraka or a native here in England, Winnie?'

'I didn't mean to insult anybody. I just wondered. Was it a shot in the dark?'

'In a pool of water.'

'Surely not cold English water?'

'No, the warm African sort – hot water as it turns out.'

'A nightcap?'

'If you like.'

'Did you see him?'

'It wasn't like that.'

'What was it like?'

Rudy spoke: 'We were escorted everywhere by boys and girls – Burrakans are not inhibited or restrained, they're not disobliging, they're not British. The girls bathed with me and the boys with Addie.'

Winnie asked: 'Is that how it happened?'

'Roughly – I mean, approximately.'

'Once?'

'I lost count.'

'Was it fun?'

'Yes, it was.'

Viv said: 'You were always honest, Addie, I admire you for that.'

Zac chimed in: 'I admire you, Addie, not only for that.'

And Rudy said: 'Hear, hear!'

Phil, too, had something to say.

'What I'd like,' she said, 'is that nobody else goes anywhere for as long as possible. We've lost Noah for ever, and Magda probably ditto, and Rudy's been abroad for ages, and Addie and Zac have only just come home – couldn't we all sit down and be together quietly now?'

143

The siblings laughed. There was further questioning of Zac; but his answers were terse, he was so much more head than body, he was not suspected of having done much in the sexual connection.

Phil's plea for at least a period of *status quo ante* fell on deaf ears, Addie's ears in particular. She was the more embarrassed by her size as the months passed. She could not tell the truth and hated having to tell lies. She was helped by her father to rent a flatlet in London and become the patient of Dr Matthews.

Notwithstanding her distress throughout her pregnancy she gave birth to three small but healthy male babies. They were identically brown, but one had a sensitive protruding back to his head, another an insensitive lack of protrusion, and the third big ears. Moreover one had a snub nose, another a nose that was sharp, and the third no nose to speak of. That each looked different from the others was only to be expected, Addie reflected. Anyway, she loved them all, and could feed them without stinting. She called them William, Thomas and James.

Her return to Castle Scar was sweet and sour. Her mother was delighted to have three more babies to attend to, her father was not hostile, her siblings were intrigued and loyal; but then the buts began.

Three illegitimate children in the Hope family was hot news locally, and their colour was more than a nine days wonder. They were not only instant celebrities, they would continue to be so, and bad boys of every age, at school and in later life, would throw brickbats at them. Addie's vague fears were realised. Where were the four of them to live? She could not stay at home for the next twenty-odd years, it would not be good for her parents, it would be bad for her. What about money? She would have to get into remunerative work without delay: but how, and who would be mother then? She sometimes allowed regrets and foresight to pose a threat to her constitution, a temporary threat, for she definitely could not afford to weaken or fall ill. The absolution she at last sought from Father O'Malley, although it did not wipe the slate clean, encouraged her to recover faith in her religion.

A few years passed. It was summer again at Castle Scar. The six siblings were gathered together on the terrace at teatime, Winnie, Phil, Rudy, Zac and Viv, also Addie. The latter had been living in London, where she had a job in a publishing house. She had raised her boys with help from all and sundry, and had brought them down to Cornwall for a holiday. Now, her William, Thomas and James were with Winnie's Peter on the beach, and their grandmother Mary was in charge of them. Edward was snipping away with his secateurs in the garden.

The sun shone on the Band of Hope, the distant cries of the children in the sea reached them, the cream cake for tea had been eaten, and the pleasures of the senses minimised the effect of Rudy's grim picture of life on our planet in the future and on the British Isles in particular.

Statistics, he said, were pointing at unmanageable over-population, shortages of food and fresh water, not enough energy to light or heat our houses, cook our meals, run our means of transport, and then pandemics compounded by crime and wars, wars without end.

'If you think I'm peddling doom,' he said, 'remember the recent past. In the first third of this twentieth century, in the thirty-odd years of it, we've had the Great War, the Russian revolution, Fascism in Italy and Nazism in Germany. In the next two thirds, and in the year two thousand and in the two thousandth century, our politicians will surely serve up more blood, more misery, tragedies rendered more tragic by modern inventions, and cruelty likewise. And I speak only for our European corner of the world – other corners will no doubt make their contribution to the history of catastrophe. What's the answer, what's the remedy? I have one, a counsel of despair. The silent majority, in the days ahead, will be more silent, because they are up against the irresistible forces of destiny and decay. Every man and every woman, and every politician too, will seek satisfaction in drugs. The masses will be sedated, so that the politicians will not have to fear revolt and reckoning. The characters featured in the old story, the story older than mine, were John Barleycorn and Milady Nicotine, and hashish, laudanum, opiates of various types. In Africa, where I lived and Zac and Addie came to be with me, another drug is on offer. Saha, the Burrakan drink, has no harmful side-effects consumed in moderation, and, combined with the smack of wise and firm government, creates a beautiful society. People are happy and healthy, thanks to saha, and good – it changed the three of us for the better, didn't it?'

Addie and Zac agreed.

Rudy continued: 'I'm saying nothing new, other people have said it before me, but perhaps I can say it again with more urgency. Saha made me see not the light at the end of our tunnel, but the terrible future in store for us. People will have to take drugs to stand it. Governments will sanction drug addiction. Science must work hard and fast, while there is still a window of opportunity, to invent a drug as beneficial as saha. Yes, I found what I was looking for in Africa, something more up to date than tyranny and despotism, futuristic, if you like, the panacea that could cure the mess we have made and are making of our world.'

Rudy was disagreed with. He had put his head on the block and Winnie and Viv took turns at trying to chop it off. Britain was still great, Winnie claimed, it was certainly not a mess compared with Africa, it never would or could be so bad as Rudy prophesied, and the idea of it turning into a kind of opium den was unpatriotic. Viv found fault with Burraka, an obviously undemocratic state. He said that Rudy seemed to have been robbed there of his dedication to the cause of the individual's human rights. Moreover, speaking personally, and with apologies

147

for being his brother's candid friend, he was pretty disgusted to think of Rudy behaving like a breeding bull; and he was not overjoyed to discover his close relationship with even a small percentage of the born and unborn Burrakan population.

Addie intervened. At length she had a chance to teach the lesson she had learned in Burraka – teach not her siblings, she was well aware that it was too late for that, no, she was just keen to pass on her wishful thinking and compassion for young women in the future.

She said: 'There must be a better female contraceptive. Viv, you're a scientist, invent one, please! Every device obtainable today is uncomfortable, unreliable, unattractive. Can't there be a pill? I'm guessing a pill will be available one day – one fine day for women, and for men, too, a really practical and popular scientific advance for a change! Rudy's right, saha seems to solve many problems, but imagine the problems a contraceptive pill would solve! No more taking your temperature before you make love, no more invasive gynaecological assistance, no more fear of babies, no more enforced chastity, not so many headaches for women and locked bedroom doors, not so many prostitutes for sex-starved husbands! Instead, love that would be free, married couples not haunted by possible responsibilities, fidelity made easy, frustration a thing of the past, a new era for women who could do as men have done, and the goal of equality achieved!'

These proposals put forward by Rudy and

Addie were argued over for days within the hearing of their parents.

Edward caught the drift of them and one evening gave Jones the benefit of a paraphrase.

'They think we should all be under the influence of drugs and women should have a foolproof contraceptive.'

'What sort of drugs are they after?'

'A new one that'll stop you feeling life's not worth living.'

'And women are wanting a pill to let them do as they please?'

'That's Addie's idea.'

'Husbands won't be pleased if their wives behave anyhow.'

'I don't think there'll be many husbands if my children have their way, not if wives can fleece hubbies with a divorce, and wives are even more difficult to trust than nature's made them.'

'Drugs and love on the cheap – will it be better than what we've got, sir?'

'Who knows? With luck, we won't, Jones.'

ZACHARIAH

Zachariah had the longest Christian name and the most elongated body of the members of the Band of Hope. He was tall and bony. He had a big bony nose and a jutting chin. He was no oil painting, the village people remarked, but they thought he looked honest. His nickname at school was 'Gawks'. His mother was convinced that he would be handsome and craggy when he was old.

His defining characteristic from boyhood onwards was unworldliness. His kindness made him especially popular within the family, also elsewhere. He was tolerant, good-humoured, showed goodwill, and was vulnerable. Nobody seemed to want to hurt his feelings, though they were tempted to tease him for taking too much too seriously. And his large blue eyes and easy smile disarmed bullies.

He was an aimless youth compared with Magda who was susceptible to power, Winnie who was a slave of fashion, Noah who believed in fishing and a false god, Phil who passionately wanted nothing, Rudy who had his African dream, and Addie who aspired to take the responsibility out of sex. Zac had no wish-list. He played dot

153

cricket and patience with himself, and mooned through life somewhat impenetrably. He had a brain, but used it for nothing except to pass exams.

At university he studied subjects that are now lumped together under the denomination of sociology. He read about poverty and the plight of people who have always been and have opted to be at the bottom of the social pile. He was interested in the physiological causes of bad luck and crime. He was too honest to embrace the theory of egalitarianism and the abolition of privilege, but amused to learn that Karl Marx read Dickens to his children, *Great Expectations* probably, which is a lyrical poem in praise of capitalism, while he – Mark – was writing about the death of capital and urging the liquidation of capitalists. He took views, he had opinions, but they were never static – he swayed in the breezes of his reading matter. His teachers in general had to face the fact that they had failed to turn a schoolboy into a scholar, yet one or two suspected that Zac might be an original.

After university, while he kicked his heels at Castle Scar and wondered what to do next, he received an invitation via his college authorities to serve on a government-sponsored committee that was to study the possible connection between housing and health.

His siblings were against acceptance: Zac was not a bureaucrat, should not get involved in futile do-gooding, would be exasperated by bores patting themselves on the back at meetings, and deserved better than to waste his substance on statistics.

But Zac accepted and was enrolled in the Cornish branch of the nationwide investigation, which met conveniently at Trepenison. He bicycled there, to the house of a Mrs Gwen Railton, who would be chairing the meeting. It went quite well. There were six of them, Gwen was about fifty – divorced – brown hair gathered up in a loose sort of bun – full of good works, and mother of a daughter, Caroline, who was being 'finished' at a school in Paris. She volunteered her autobiographical facts in a strong voice. Stephen, Vicky, Nicky, who was female, and Molly, the other volunteers, were nondescript and amenable.

Gwen was clearly impressed by Zac's academic qualifications and sought his advice on every point at issue. They smiled at each other, but did not stray from the sociological context. A second meeting was scheduled for a fortnight ahead. At it, the attendance was four, Stephen and Vicky had dropped out. And at the third meeting Gwen and Zac were by themselves, and agreed that they accomplished far more than would have been the case with amateurish interruptions.

Zac liked Gwen. He approved of her brisk approach to problems. He soon thought of her as a friend and a reliable person. He enjoyed her admiration of his analytical powers and ability to extract the essential elements from sheafs of paper blackened with lists, numbers, headings,

155

capitals and italics. He began to stay for tea at her modest house, Swallows, and on one occasion had a cosy dinner beside a log fire in the lounge. He paid her back by asking her to tea at Castle Scar, but that did not go so well – his siblings chose to be stand-offish.

For Zac, Caroline Railton added an extra pleasure to his association with Gwen. Caroline returned from Paris looking like an advertisement for Parisian *chic*. She was nineteen, a pretty blonde, and wore clothes that even Zac could see were as smart as un-English paint. She had a sweet smile, too, and the shape of it, of her white strong teeth, and pale pink moist hint of gums, made a deep impression.

At a tea at Swallows Caroline was present, and she and Zac shared a joke or two and had a giggle together. He was attracted for the first time in his life. He was a slow developer, in his twenty-fourth year he was at last aware of a mild pang of love. It confused him. It raised him out of his rut, which had been a peaceful place to be. He thought of Caroline instead of statistics. He thought of her lips, teeth, and the healthy cleanliness of both. His thoughts were more objective than personal, kisses were altogether out of range, he regarded her rather as a work of art, rare and beautiful art.

One summer's afternoon, following an industrious lunch with Gwen at Swallows, Zac met Caroline out in the roadway. They were both wheeling bicycles, he was preparing to bicycle back to Castle Scar, she said she was bicycling to the seaside for a swim – she had a towel rolled up in her carrier-bag. He hesitated, recalling that Phil had had trouble with Nigel Wallace-East in similar circumstances; but he banished the recollection, Nigel was nasty and Phil neurotic. He invited Caroline to bathe at his family's semi-private beach. They bicycled there, he led her through the garden and down the zigzag path, and she divested herself of her outer garments, and in her red swimsuit ran into the sea. He watched her, he seldom swam. He sat and loved her for waving at him and laughing, and for seeming to have a body as supple as a fish. When she rejoined him he handed her the towel, and asked if she would like to dry herself up at the Castle.

Oh no, she said, she was not in a fit state to meet his people, she would dry in the sun, and she was having such a nice time.

She lay on the towel beside him, now shaking the sand out of her golden hair, now turning over – 'like a piece of toast,' she said; and they talked. But it was not talking as Zac had known it, not the clash of opinions with siblings, not confessional chats with Father O'Malley; he had the idea that he was communing with Caroline.

She broke down barriers with her artless and almost childish questions and confidences. How old was he, did he have lots of girlfriends, had it been difficult to be one of eight children, was he a churchy Catholic? She was an only child, was disillusioned by her father who had deserted her and married again and had two other children, was shy with men whom she could not completely trust, was miles apart from her mother, and sometimes lonely although she had her dreams.

'What do you dream about?' Zac heard himself asking – he had never asked any girl such an intimate question.

'What do you think?' She laughed, they both did. 'What do you think girls dream about?'

'Love, I suppose.'

'And happiness. Don't you dream of those things?'

'I don't know.'

'Oh you're so funny,' she laughed. 'You'll have to watch out, not knowing could get you into trouble. What does Zac mean?'

'It's short for Zachariah, he was a king of Israel – in the Bible, the Old Testament.'

'You're like a king.'

'Am I?'

'And the cliff and this beach is your country.'

'Not mine, no – yours today.'

'You're flattering me. I'd rather you were honest.'

'Oh ... Are you dry now?'

'Yes,' she sighed; 'so I'll have to get up and go.'

'Won't you stay to tea?'

'No – please don't ask.'

'Why?'

'I don't want to spoil our time.'

They climbed up the path, she reaching out a hand, he taking it and pulling her up the steeper bits. At the top she asked him if they could be friends.

He mumbled a reply, he was too touched to speak. She smiled at him and bicycled away.

He could not believe it. He could scarcely believe it had happened. He did know something about love now – he had never imagined the company of a girl could be so delightful as his couple of hours with Caroline Railton had been. He was a different person, almost crowned, in fact, by the favour of a member of the opposite sex. His feelings for her were, or seemed to be, pure and spiritual, even if they verged on religious heresy. They lifted his spirits, and simultaneously introduced uncertainty into the realm of wishes and possibilities. Would she spend more time with him? How was their friendship to develop?

Some days later he had an appointment with Gwen. They were to meet at six o'clock and try to unite various statistical conclusions they had separately reached. Zac bicycled along roads hallowed by Caroline's bicycle. He was in an excited state, looking forward to confiding in the mother and seeing the daughter. He was greeted by Gwen, who led him straight into the kitchen. Piles of typescript, sheets of paper, pencils and rubbers were laid out on one end of the table, and two trays laid with cutlery and glasses at the other end.

Zac asked: 'Are the trays for you and Caroline?' He was confused, his question struck him as impertinent as soon as it was out of his mouth.

'They're for us,' Gwen replied. 'I was hoping you'd stay on and have supper with me.'

'Oh,' he said. 'Oh yes, thanks, I'd like that.'

'Good. Now to work! Sit on that chair!'

He did as he was told. He sensed that he was under pressure and perhaps that he should steer clear of the subject of Caroline. But he could not resist the temptation to speak her name.

'Is Caroline here?' he asked.

'No, she's left.'

'She didn't say she was leaving. We met the other day. She had a swim off the Scar beach.'

'So I heard. It was kind of you to let her swim there.'

'Where's she gone?'

'She's staying with an aunt of mine, her great-aunt, who's poorly, for the foreseeable future.'

'Where's that?'

'I am not going to answer your question. She's very young, and needs to do some useful work.'

'I see. Actually, Gwen, I don't see. Caroline and I are friends. I wouldn't like her to think I've forgotten her.'

'Zac, listen! Caroline's a silly young girl and not a suitable friend for a man with your intelligence and your distinguished future in the offing. You've been leading each other up garden paths. She saw the point of my arguments, and I trust you will. Now, for heaven's sake, to work! Shall we get down to what has to be done?'

Zac cooperated. He felt himself drifting far out to sea. Had Caroline not been frank with him? Was Gwen lying for some reason?

The statistics took precedence. Zac worked with, or for, Gwen Railton for an hour or so. Then she served a supper of cold salmon with

160

trimmings, followed by strawberries and cream, cheese and coffee, accompanied by white wine. They had carried their trays into the sitting-room and placed them on occasional tables. They sat side by side to eat and drink. When they finished, she lifted the trays on to the floor, took hold of his available hand, stroked it, and treated him to a little lecture.

'Honestly, dear Zac, Caroline wouldn't do for you. Somebody's heart would be broken sooner or later. She could never interest a man with intellectual preoccupations, and how would you do your work with babies bawling and keeping you awake at night? I understand you as she never would, and I believe it's my turn to teach you something, gratefully and fondly. Why not? Fair exchange is no robbery, isn't that so?'

Before he could answer, and because he was not sure how to, she kissed him on the lips. She leant across and gave him a great bite that bore no resemblance to the kisses he had received and given for twenty-four years. It scared. It disgusted. He pushed or pulled away, mumbling apologies.

'Don't,' she scolded. 'Sit still! Let me help you grow up! Relax now, relax and come to my bed.'

'What? No! What ... Sorry ... I must go.'

He struggled up, out of her grasp, and made for the door.

'Think over the offer, Zac,' she called after him.

'Oh yes – no – thank you – good night!'

He was miserable on his bike. He had made a fool of himself. He had been a coward to flee from a woman. He had been an ass not to realise she had designs on his body as well as his mind. She was a carnivore in statistician's clothing. Women were not like his sisters. Gwen had undergone a transformation for the worse. And Caroline, his friend, the work of art, had left him in the lurch, had not let him know she was being punished for having won his heart. Trust had been betrayed all round. His preference for the daughter had caused the mother to shut up a young girl with a sick great-aunt in the frozen north. The way of the world was unjust and painful – and he was somehow to blame.

The consequence was Burraka. Almost as he reached Castle Scar on the unhappy evening of his first proper or improper kiss, Addie was talking of her expedition in search of Rudy in Africa. Would he accompany her? Would he be her guardian angel? The chance he was offered, and its timing, were like deliverance.

Yet during the voyage out, then in the bizarre African geography, in deserts in the roasting heat and amongst the flies, he could not stop thinking of the Railtons and their offers that he had allowed to slip through his fingers. Caroline might have become the love of his life, Gwen's kiss might have been page one of a sexual encyclopaedia. The maddening thing was that he realised Gwen had been right about his possible future with her daughter, if for the wrong reason, because she wanted him for herself. Besides, he could not marry even a girl with the most seductive of lips and teeth, he was not ready, he did not possess enough of the 'ready', moreover the work he contemplated, the great worthwhile work, was as yet unformed and unidentified. At the same time he shrank from the imaginary image of Gwen undressed, with wobbly breasts and thighs like hams.

Rudy's life-style in Burraka was salt in the wounds of Zac. Of course he disapproved of Rudy's public orgasms, under water though they were, they were dead against manners, morality and Catholicism; on the other hand he was curious, excited, and refrained from outspoken criticism. Addie scarcely scolded Rudy, they were all drinking saha, and in time, inevitably, Zac succumbed to temptation. The brown nymphs who escorted him into the warm water of the palatial pool looked to him like Caroline Railton in the moonlight, and their caresses were Caroline's. Later on, the brothers' discovery of Addie's participation in the rites of the pool, observed without her knowing it, added to their pleasure and subtracted from their guilt. But when she recalled them to duty and Castle Scar, Rudy remembered his loose ends in England and Zac was glad.

They withstood the family's adverse reactions to their account, the bowdlerized version, of the African adventure, and Zac soon committed himself and his future to the penance of hard labour in his particular field. For the time being he shut sex out – it was not too difficult as a matter of fact. He was happy again, metaphorically buried in books, and haunting record offices, libraries, church registers and hospital accounts. His family had thought him idle, some members of it had said so, but now they begged him to rest his eyes and not to rush into a nervous breakdown. He lived at home and rented rooms in b-and-bs in cities, towns and villages where he could find his version of treasure-trove.

For a year, then another year and a third, he would answer none of the questions fired at him by his siblings. However, when his work had reached a debatable stage, he summoned a meeting of all the adult and surviving members of his family, parents included. It took place at six o'clock on an evening in November in the living-room with the chapel attached and its long view of the Atlantic Ocean. The Penzootes sat in their customary armchairs on either side of the fire, Mary on the right, Edward on the left. Zac sat in an upright chair next to his mother, and had no papers or notes handy. The others were scattered on sofas and on the floor, Winnie sat with Phil on the floor, leaning back against the legs of brothers.

Zac began: 'I've been working out a plan to improve the health of all and sundry.'

The interruptions were: 'But you're not a doctor ... What are your qualifications? ... Is God in our midst?'

Zac was asked to explain.

'We'd be the patients of the government, and we'd be treated free,' he said.

The immediate objections were, first, that Whitehall is the home of errors, secondly, that nothing organised by government was free, we would be paying higher taxes for the government to fritter away.

'Poor people can't afford doctors and hospital bills,' Zac retorted. 'Wealthy people would probably have to pay a little more tax, but they'd be treated by doctors without having to pay anything.'

Was Zac organising yet another charity, a mammoth charity? And what would happen to the wonderful cottage hospital in Trepenison, which only charged patients what they could afford to pay, and was otherwise financed by local fund-raising events – would our hospital be run by faceless civil servants in London?

'It would not be charity, there could be an insurance scheme to pay for it, a national insurance policy for the whole population.' Zac added that he was aware of people not liking to think they were living on charity. He continued: 'About our cottage hospital, the scheme might be voluntary, our hospital could opt out.'

Loud objections: he was juggling words, charity and a national insurance policy were synonymous, Zac would soon be calling the money we would have to fork out for his scheme 'investment', although it boiled down to giving our money to the government to spend on a so-called good cause of its choice. Furthermore, it was a hoary old joke that authoritative calls for 'volunteers' were orders, also a threat that refusals to 'volunteer' would be punished.

Zac countered: 'My scheme would be a step in the direction of equality of opportunity.'

'Yes, but...' they said.

Phil chipped in: 'I'm afraid it would be a great change. I mean Dr Hopkinson wouldn't be able to look after us, he'd be filling in government forms all day, and we'd be one of your statistics.'

Viv also had something to say: 'Our country's overcrowded, even after the war there are too many of us, and in peacetime we'll multiply. Furthermore, science is going to be able to prolong our lives, those are ineluctable facts, Zac, so how do you think your scheme will work in the future, when it's in charge of the health of fifty or sixty or more million people, when it's responsible for their welfare and could be sued for failing to keep them healthy, and when the cost of it all doubles or trebles because of all the new medical advances?'

'Our country might be richer then,' Zac replied.

'One fine day, you mean?'

'Yes, if you like, one day which could be finer than days are for ill people nowadays.'

Winnie intervened: 'I'd qualify as a poor person to get my Peter's adenoids removed.'

Addie said: 'Well, I'll have doctor's bills for my three. I'd be in favour of free medicines and stuff.'

Rudy put his oar in: 'I'm planning not to be here when you get your scheme off the ground, Zac – I'll be in Africa. I therefore shouldn't comment, but I belong to the Band of Hope so of course I will. I'm thanking my stars that I won't have to pay through the nose to finance your effort to do good.'

166

A chorus of voices sought the opinion of Edward: 'What do you think, Father?'

Edward asked Zac: 'Are you in touch with other people who share your ideas?'

Zac answered in the affirmative, a group of Cambridge academics and a committee of politicians were separately looking into the possibility of medical services on the state.

Edward commented, 'I wish you well,' and refused to be drawn further into the argument.

But some days later he provided Jones with a thumbnail sketch of Zac's intentions.

'Be pricey, wouldn't it?' Jones inquired.

'I expect so.'

'Good for some, though.'

'True.'

'Treat everybody, do the doctoring for everyone, is that what he says?'

'Just about.'

'That'll take a lot of paperwork.'

'And people won't be grateful long term, they'll complain instead of saying thanks.'

VIVIAN

Viv was the youngest and strangest of the eight strange children of Lord and Lady Penzoote. He was born with a lot of hair and it was black. He had a fair complexion, blue-green eyes, and black hair, a striking combination. He also exuded a strong personality. Visitors to Castle Scar, and acquaintances met in the village street or in Trepenison, who looked into his cot or pram, were startled by the intense glare of the baby with his vivid colouring. They almost recoiled.

He made deep and immediate impressions. Mary, his mother, accustomed as she was to bearing clever children, guessed at once that Viv might turn out to be cleverer than the other seven. She called him after a great-great-uncle of hers, who had invented a superior muck-spreader. He was good-humoured and humorous, but occasionally moody, and sometimes independent to the point of being withdrawn. He amused his siblings, and won their respect. Although he was only a year younger than Zac, and two years younger than Addie, the feeling was – the feeling of the whole family – that he belonged to a generation of his own.

He was rather a nuisance before he went to

171

school. He asked too many questions. He was relentlessly inquisitive. But then he became the favourite of his intelligent teachers and simultaneously the despair of teachers more interested in obedience, discipline and handwriting. He was quick on the uptake, and grateful for being taught. On the other hand his black hair outgrew the barber's scissors, his head resembled a mop, and he was incorrigibly inky – he could not control his fountain pen, he always had ink on his fingers and face. He was apt to break rules because he was not interested in them, and to be impolite through absent-mindedness. He was no good at games, he was a butter-fingers until someone realised that he needed spectacles. His school-fellows called him names, 'bookworm' and 'swot', but they kept their distance on the whole and resigned themselves to his streaking ahead of them in class.

He gravitated into the whirlpool of exams. He crammed for one, passed it, crammed for another, and so it went on. His mother was torn between pride and anxiety, proud of his attainments and sure that he was ruining his eyesight and his health. His father was also concerned, although happy not to have to pay school fees. Viv won scholarships, prizes, letters after his name, reputation. While he studied post-graduate work precociously he was invited to join a select group of researchers. The family was not neglectful of his academic success and renown; but nobody had much to say on the subject because no family members had any knowledge of what he was renowned for. He was first a mathematician and then a physicist. His siblings excelled at English, history, philosophy, languages, and, in the case of Winnie, cooking. His siblings did not do sums. And Viv could or would not explain. He was especially secretive about those hieroglyphics he was inclined to scribble on scraps of paper. He half-hinted that the work of research in which he would be involved was hush-hush.

Considering his talent for maths, it was at least ironical that he should be the only member of the Band of Hope to prove himself hopeless with money. He was well into the age of discretion when he informed his father that he was in debt and about to be bankrupt. The capital sum that Edward had set aside for each of his children had gone west, and Viv had also spent a lot more than his annual income from grants, bursaries, gifts from his father and earnings from book reviews and lectures.

'What have you spent it on?' Edward inquired.
'I don't know.'
'You must know. Concentrate – have you lashed out on wild women and song?'
'Oh Father!'
'What then?'
'Here's my statement from the bank.'
Edward read it. Every item was a payment by cheque to a charitable organisation. But the organisations were even more worrying than the money they had received. They were called Safe Homes for Dogs in Korea, Support a Donkey in the Sudan, African Orphans, Carnival Costumes

for Rio de Janeiro, and Distressed Gentlewomen of Russia. Some of the charities were not registered and must have been run by lunatics or crooks.

Edward said to Viv: 'My dear boy, they eat dogs in Korea, donkeys in Sudan don't stand much of a chance, African orphans are the tip of a needy iceberg in that hot country, costumes in the Rio carnival are so scant that your donation would do for the entire population of the city, and gentlewomen are thin on the ground everywhere and I can't believe many have survived the attentions of Lenin's and Stalin's death squads.'

Viv laughed.

'Don't laugh, but don't worry. I'll save your bacon. Why did you support such peculiar causes, lost causes?'

Vivian laughed again and said: 'I thought they were funny.'

'Well, think again if you ever have any more money in your account.'

'Thanks, Father – I will.'

Shortly after the monetary crises Viv tried to commit suicide. More accurately, he walked across the lawn to the edge of the scar, meaning to jump on to the rocks below. More accurately still, he was having a mental seizure, the start of a nervous breakdown, and had reasons that were not rational.

Drama reigned in the Castle. Jones had rescued Viv. Jones had been making a late evening inspection of the garden – like all gardeners, he fancied he was being robbed of his flowers; he had seen the figure poised on the edge of the scar, seized hold of a possible thief, and recognised Master Vivian, whom he then led home, through the open French windows and into the sitting-room to which the family had adjourned after dinner.

When the hubbub of anxious questions had subsided, Viv tried to explain himself.

'I wouldn't have come to harm,' he said, 'because I would have spread my wings.'

What wings, they asked: who did he think he was?

'Not who,' he replied.

Had he thought he was a bird?

'Not a bird,' he replied.

An angel?

'No – a bat.'

At this point Mary escorted Viv upstairs, put him to bed in the twin-bedded spare room, gave him two aspirins to swallow, and summoned Zac from downstairs to sleep in the same room with his brother, after pushing furniture across the window and locking the door.

Viv had recovered by morning. He was able to apologise to everyone for the previous evening's performance, and he added a twist to references to bats: 'Bats in my belfry!' His siblings worked out how much, or rather how little, sleep he had had in the last few weeks, and counted the number of books he had studied in the same period, papers he had written, committee meetings attended, and cross-country journeys he had made. No wonder his mind had taken a night off, they said. Mary said Viv was run down and ordered a specially nourishing lunch. Edward said Viv would be okay soon.

However, Viv fretted over his loss of grip and self-control. He was well aware of students suffering the effects of overwork, experiences similar to his own, but he was proud enough in spite of his modesty to have thought he was above that sort of thing. Moreover, he was a scientist and wanted to know how and why his brain, his powerful and protective brain, had failed him without warning. He felt he could not devote himself to his work and carry on as before until this most annoying of all his problems was solved.

For once he was open with his family: he asked them for advice. His mother suggested Dr Hopkinson in the village; Winnie a handsome masseur she was friendly with; Phil recommended rest; Rudy favoured alcohol; Addie muttered the word psychology, and Zac was for Harley Street.

Viv opted for a Professor Freundberg. He was a doctor and a psychologist, as his name suggested Austrian, and had studied the works and methods of Sigmund Freud. Novelty is a magnet for scientists, and Viv was drawn to the new science of treating the mind as well as the body of man, and hoped the Professor could throw light on his uncharacteristic behaviour. His siblings were also curious to know more about psychology.

He made an appointment and reported to a small detached Edwardian type of house in Hampstead. A starchy nurse of the Brunhilde build with a teutonic accent ushered him into a

waiting-room. In time a woman who had undergone psychology staggered in, crying, collected
a coat lying on a chair, and staggered out. Then
the nurse ushered Viv into the Professor's consulting room.

It was very gloomy. Thick net curtain shut
out the afternoon sunshine. Everything seemed
to be brown, a roll-top desk, a couch with false
leather covering, the wallpaper, the carpet. The
Professor was large and stout, bearded, wearing
pince-nez, attired in an old-fashioned stick-up
shirt-collar, a black bow-tie and a brown pinstripe
three-piece suit. He greeted Vivian with a two-
handed handshake and a smile that showed some
teeth capped with gold. He sat at his desk, Viv
on an adjacent chair. He asked questions and
wrote down the answers. In due course he asked
Vivian to lie down on the couch and the analytical
treatment began.

A full account of it was retailed to Viv's family
on his return to Castle Scar. He mimicked
Professor Freundberg's guttural delivery and
mocked the whole rigmarole with the accuracy
of his recollections and objectivity. First, there
had been a session of free association: the Professor
said cheese, pencil, motorcar etc, and Viv replied
cheddar, Venus, Rolls-Royce, then complained
that the exchanges were babyish.

'Ach so!' Professor Freundberg exclaimed.
'Babyish for you, sir, maybe, but for me very
interesting.'

He referred in sanctimonious accents to his
great teacher, the neurologist Sigmund Freud,

then asked a direct question: 'If I say to you the word "father", what do you say to me?'

'I say, what are you talking about?'

'That is not the answer. I think you are hiding from me.'

'Hiding? I'm not hiding, I'm lying on this couch of yours.'

'It is good that you are not pleased with me. I think I have touched the sensitive spot.'

'Well, I am getting less pleased all the time. Is that more than good?'

'Would you wish to kill your father?'

'I beg your pardon?'

'Mother!'

'Excuse me?'

'I said the word "mother".'

'Do you mean you are calling out for your mother?'

'I think you are hiding from me again.'

'Professor Freundberg, use your eyes, I am lying here large as life within four feet of yourself.'

'You are not fond of your mother?'

'Yes, I am, of course I am. Weren't you fond of yours?'

'Ach so, very interesting.'

'What are you driving at, Professor Freundberg?'

'You thought you were a bat?'

'Momentarily, yes. I probably had a few moments of not knowing who or what I was. But luckily no harm came of it. I'm here to find out if you and your psychoanalysis can throw any light on my experience.'

'Analysis is not over in time for luncheon.'

'How long does it take?'

'Years, often many years.'

'I'm sorry, Professor. I have work to do. I am a physicist. I have no years to spare.'

'A physicist, that is not a joke, is it?'

'Certainly not. Is psychoanalysis a joke? It seems to be quite laughable.'

'Laughable, that is funny! Ha ha!'

'Professor, our time is money.'

'Ach so! You wish me to give you a cheap rate?'

'What do you have to tell me? What is your diagnosis?'

'God.'

'Are you saying I am or think I am God?'

'You believe in God?'

'I do, I'm a Christian.'

'You are pining for your infancy.'

'I am not.'

'You are obsessed with your mother.'

'Tommy-rot!'

'You have the Oedipus complex.'

'And you are levelling wild accusations at me! Is this the Freudian treatment?'

'I accuse you of nothing. Nothing is wrong in the region of the psyche. Psychoanalysis does not recognise sin. Original sin is a devil, and devils and hell were invented to control children and the masses.'

'Professor Freundberg, that's the philosophy of wickedness. You sanction great crimes with such nostrums. I don't think much of your Sigmund Freud. Good day!'

Viv's description of pulling himself up to his

full height and shaking the dust of the Professor's premises from his feet concluded with his being metaphorically collared by the German nurse on the way out and charged twenty-five quid.

Oddly enough, his session with Professor Freundberg was more therapeutic than he had thought it. And his probably satirical story of the psychoanalysis, and the amusement it caused, marked his return to health and a more professional rearrangement of his expenditure of energy. He worked within the limits of his strength, mental and physical, and spent regular rest periods at Castle Scar after study at Cambridge.

Another odd feature of Viv's recovery from his moment of madness was its connection or disconnection with the political news. Adolf Hitler, Chancellor of Germany, was rousing the rabble with his speeches. Those melodramatic rants, and those military charades, which had undone Magda Hope, were being taken seriously not only by a weak-minded English debutante. The German people were bewildered by defeat in the 1914 war, by runaway inflation and industrial slump; and what was Hitler to do with all the men he had dressed in smart uniforms and given guns to play with? The answer to that question looked like war. Memories united with common sense to spread alarm in the countries close to the coven of Nazism. Pressure mounted on European nerves and constitutions, on European optimism and complacence, weakened by the accumulating evidence of the barbaric inclinations of the Bolsheviks in Russia.

Edward Penzoote shook his head over his morning newspaper. Mary, in rare gaps in her busy schedule, asked fearful questions: for instance, should they keep a cow to provide them with milk and butter in the event of war and rationing? Mary and the rest of her family began to worry about the Waxmann contingent. The exception was Viv. He had put on weight and turned into a man of striking appearance with his black hair and eyebrows and glowing red cheeks. He was also more forthcoming, witness the playlet he enacted to illustrate the impracticality of psycho-analysis. The one area subject to his typical reserve was his activity in Cambridge. If he was engaged in post-graduate studies, his siblings asked from time to time, where was his thesis and where was his doctorate?

Edward Penzoote went to London: his journey was so unwonted as to merit a mention. He said he was going to buy a big umbrella against a rainy day – a reference to the investment of money and its conservation. On his return to Castle Scar he informed everyone, barring the relevant person, that he had met a man who knew a man who knew Viv and had said that he was engaged in work of universal importance.

Viv arrived home and was now beset with demands for information. He supplied it. His reason for supplying it was not the curiosity of his family, but a recent article in a learned journal – the cat was out of the bag, in other words. He said his piece over drinks before dinner on a Friday afternoon in summer. Again the French

181

windows were open and the cries of young bathers in the sea below were audible.

Viv said: 'I'll be brief, and won't bother you with a lecture on physics you wouldn't understand. I'm in a team that's studying the possibility of splitting the atom.'

He then said, laughing: 'Blank faces! I'll explain. But first I'd like to thank Father for helping to keep me alive while I'm doing this work on almost a voluntary and unpaid basis. I wouldn't have accepted your money, Father, if I hadn't been convinced that my work is worth something, and could be of great value, I mean of great value to our race and poor people everywhere. You don't understand yet – why should you? I'm talking high physics, the highest of the high. The atom split releases energy of previously unimaginable power. That power is what we're looking for, dreaming of, aspiring to obtain, in order to transform the economics of the world, the agriculture of the world, the daily life of people, and in principle their improved chances of health and happiness.'

'Goodness me, darling,' Mary exclaimed. 'Big ideas,' Zac remarked sceptically. Winnie said, 'Congrats, Viv,' and Addie, 'Are you my little brother?' Rudy said: 'I'll help myself to another drink. Anybody else want one?'

'Go on,' Edward said.

'I'll give you a few random examples of the potential benefits of our having at our disposal the power unleashed by splitting the atom: cheap light, heat and food; sea water desalinated at affordable expense, fresh water available to turn deserts into farms and gardens; an end to our dependence on oil and gas and coal; means of mobility on offer at low prices; the hard labour of producing fossil fuels like coal replaced by a finger on a button; life expectancy lengthened; medical resources improved.'

'The other side of the medal, please,' Edward requested.

'What's your particular question, Father?'

'In a war?'

'Yes, well, that's the best bit of the story. Atomic fission could be a bomb. It could be a bigger bomb than any we've known. And it could protect us. It could stop war. If we succeed, and when we know more than we do at present, we'll publicise the amount of damage an atomic bomb would do, and then no country would dare to risk having one dropped on it.'

'A pacifist bomb,' Zac said in an aside.

'Are other physicists in other countries doing work similar to yours?' Edward asked.

'I believe so.'

'Which countries?'

'America.'

'Germany?'

'Yes.'

'Who's ahead?'

'We are, I think.'

'When will you have a bomb ready to drop on our enemies?'

Everyone laughed.

'It's not like that, Father,' Viv replied.

'But it is – we all have a vested interest in knowing roughly when you'll be able to stop a war.'

'Roughly, ten years.'

'Is that a firm date?'

'I can't be sure.'

'Nineteen forty-four, roughly.'

'I think so.'

'Better be sure, dear boy.'

At that point the gong was struck. It had been bought in a charity sale by Edward and installed in the hall of the Castle. The deep sound reverberated through the house, indicating that dinner was ready.

Mary said: 'Oh that gave me a jump! I hate the gong, Edward. Do we have to have it? It sounds like a knell.'

Winnie did not dine at Castle Scar that evening, she had to fetch Peter from the beach. Addie was also absent, she had to hurry back to her three brown babes. And Phil was too upset to take solid food after listening to Viv's aim to change the face of the earth. Only Zac and Viv himself kept their parents company, and continued to discuss atomic energy so far as they were able.

The next day, on the Saturday morning, Father O'Malley held a service in the chapel of Castle Scar – services in the chapel were regularly held on Saturdays, on Sundays Father O'Malley was too busy in his church. The whole family attended, children included, no one stayed away for any reason, no doubt because they wished to pray

184

for guidance over the controversial matter of Viv's revelations.

In the evening of that Saturday Edward strolled through his garden as shadows lengthened and birds sang and twittered sleepily. His steps led him towards Jones' cottage and soon the two old friends talked for a few minutes over the picket fence.

'Vivian's been telling us what he's up to,' Edward said.

'What's that?'

'He's trying to split the atom.'

'Oh, ah?'

'That means getting our hands on power galore.'

'Well I never!'

'It'll make life better for all of us, if he and his friends can do the job in ten years or thereabouts.'

'A lot can happen in ten years, sir.'

'Each of my children thinks he or she knows how to make life better.'

'So they do, and it's good of them, I'm sure.'

'They'd make it better, if they could, or worse.'

'That's true, better in one way, worse in another. What's wrong with Master Vivian's idea?'

'It can kill us all as well as curing us.'

'Can it now!'

'What do you think, Jones?'

'I don't think too much, sir.'

'You're right. What's the weather going to do tomorrow?'

'Fine, sir, with luck.'

MARY

Mary Penzoote could conceive no more children after Viv was born. She and her husband were not old at the time in question. Yet somehow tiredness was apt to replace wakefulness when they went to bed. They had been used to procreation. Sex for sex's sake was less exciting. Gradually and by tacit consent one relationship evolved into another.

It was 1938, four years after the outburst of self-expression of the members of the Band of Hope. Mary was approaching her fifties and Edward his retirement age – which was a joke between them because he had done no obviously remunerative work since he was wounded in the war. She was a handsome woman with a sweet expression – brown hair greying and cut shortish and neat, smile friendly with good teeth, extremely active, and maternal almost to a fault. Edward gave her a birthday present of a golden retriever puppy, Prince by name, and, when age had taught him manners, he became her shadow – they were inseparable. Prince was her prince, but her husband remained her king. She respected him and let him have the last word, at least that was always her intention. Marriage apart, motherhood was her vocation, her pleasure, her reason for being, and children, her own and others', were her reward.

Magda, her first-born, seemed at last to be making the best of a bad job. She had never come home after the Hitler business, she was afraid of possible publicity in the first place, and then ashamed of her shotgun marriage to Waxmann. Mary had taken a step towards reunion by travelling out to Germany and staying for a week in a hotel near the small Waxmann house in Berlin. She longed to see her daughter again, and meet her two grandchildren, Fritz and Christine.

It was a qualified success, Magda seemed to be the same as ever, handsome, benevolent, naïve yet no fool, and at the same time different, nervous, apprehensive. Heinrich Waxmann was bald, tubby and kind, and Fritz and Christine were sturdy – Heinrich called them his 'dumplings'. Heinrich was still a bureaucratic doctor, but no longer had anything to do with the ministries carrying out the Fuhrer's plans – he worked for the Department of Agriculture. The Waxmann house was in a suburb and had three small bedrooms. Magda and Heinrich and the children gave Mary an enthusiastic welcome.

But Magda confessed to Mary that she had been terribly homesick when she opted to stay in Germany. The arrival of her children had eased that pain; unfortunately the arrival of her mother brought it back again. She also suffered from guilt, owing to her abandonment of the humane values of the Band of Hope and her confusion of power and principle; and to marrying Heinrich for convenience.

She asserted needlessly, for it was plain to see, that she had found out how lucky she was to be Heinrich's wife, and that he was her selfless husband and the devoted father of her children. After all, they were a happy family, she said, or would have been if Hitler were to drop dead or be done to death. Oh yes, she had changed her tune, she had learnt to hate Hitler as much as she had once thought she loved him. She was afraid of the future. Heinrich worked at a desk in an office, but he wore military clothing, he would be conscripted into a war and forced to fight, and goodness knew what would happen to them in that case.

Mary comforted her as best she could, but knew nothing of politics and history. Mother and daughter agreed to hope for the best. Magda's better news was that Heinrich's government department was being moved out of Berlin and into the city of Dresden. The Waxmanns would be moving there in a matter of weeks. It would be safer, Magda was sure: even if there was a war, Dresden would surely be a safer place to live than Berlin, which was bound to be bombed.

Mary returned to Castle Scar, and, in accordance with the luck of a mother of eight, the tears of one child were counterbalanced by the smiles of another. Winnie was going to be married again. Her fiancé was a French regular soldier, André Manusse, a *capitaine*. He was a charming

Anglophile in his late thirties, who had once been a military attaché at the French Embassy in London.

The circumstances of their acquaintanceship and, in a sense, courtship were not fit for public consumption. Winnie's mother never knew, and if her father suspected he did not say so. Capitaine Manusse was the third man who had made love to her at the swimming pool party in the days or rather the nights of her youth. The amazing thing, the miracle after a secular fashion, was that notwithstanding the passage of time he had traced her. He knocked on the door of her cottage in Penzoote village, Holly Cott, one afternoon. She was deeply in love with him as soon as she was sure of his identity; and he said he was. He was desirous, she was willing, both were impatient, and he even mentioned marriage in the heat of the moment. She stalled, was twice or thrice shy, and laughed at him encouragingly and ambiguously to gain time. She introduced him to Peter, when the boy returned from school, and agreed to meet André again on the next day.

She rushed to seek advice from Addie, and began by making a clean breast of the facts of the matter. She disclosed as never before to a sibling that she had been drunk, naked, had consented to being bowled like a ball in a bowling alley along the wet tiles of the swimming pool edging, and finally to events in the cubicle. Reluctantly Winnie agreed with Addie that André would have to be told that her first and her second husbands were present at the party; but

192

she could say they were the worse for drink, sozzled, and had got it into their thick heads that they had had something to do with the conception of Peter. She could add that they were bores, duds and English stick-in-the-muds, and she had given them their marching orders chop-chop. What she absolutely could not avoid saying to André, what she was honour bound to warn him about, was that she was an objector to divorced wives being paid off with pittances, and that she had done some campaigning for the rights of ex-wives – Addie allowed that she did not need to mention her recommendation of a fifty-fifty per cent split of the joint estates of husbands and wives who divorce.

For once, the path of true love ran pretty smooth. When Winnie confessed that two Englishmen had dared to think they could have sired Peter, André proved in yet another way that he was a full-blooded Latin lover.

He responded with complacence: 'Your past is of no interest for me. I am a Frenchman, my dear, and my seed is and was more powerful than the English concoction. I do not boast, but Pierre is indubitably my boy, and he shall be a Manusse when we have exchanged our golden rings.'

Just before they did so, in the Register Office in Trepenison, André himself had a confession to make. His mother was Jewish. Winnie was unmoved: she looked forward to meeting her and perhaps to a cup of chicken soup with barley.

André corrected her: 'You do not understand.

193

You will live with me in France, and Germany will be our neighbour. Adolf Hitler promises to kill all Jews. His Nazis are murdering the people of my mother's race, people with any Jewish blood in their veins. If Hitler wages war against France, he might be the victor. And if he should be victorious, I would be in danger, you too would be, and our son would not be safe, and very bad deaths could be reserved for us.'

Winnie by way of answer put her hands over her ears and kissed him.

'Thank you,' he said. 'Now I shall chase away your fear. We will live where you wish in Paris, where I work in the office of government. I am still a French soldier and I will not allow a German to pass into the beautiful capital of my country – never!'

She thanked him, and, again in Addie's company, convinced herself that the problem was solved.

'I'll love André's mother. I think I especially love the side of André that's Jewish. I feel sure that some quality in Peter is exceptional and lovable for the same reason. And, for heaven's sake, we're not at war with Germany yet! If we were, if France was, I don't believe the Germans would win it and be able to kill whoever they please, women and children. Besides, Paris is above war, like Venice and Rome. Paris is bound to be spared in any conflict. That's my thought for the day. Oh Addie, I want to be happy so badly!'

Mary said a prayer in the chapel at Castle

Scar after the Manusses had departed for their honeymoon in the south of France – Pierre, who had been Peter, was staying with his grandparents until his parents were ready to receive him in Paris. She was never short of a child to pray for. She prayed for Magda and Winnie in their foreign homes. She prayed for the soul of Noah, and begged God to forgive him if he had died for doing something wrong. Praying for Phil might be called a dead loss – Mary could not quite bring herself to ask God to stop the world spinning. She tried to explain to the Almighty that Phil was a good person inasmuch as she wanted nobody to be upset, and incidentally not to be upset herself.

She apologised to God for Rudy. His obsession with Africa had led him astray, and now it was ending in tears. He had cried when he told his family that Burraka was done for. The Italian conquest of Ethiopia had shaken the African kaleidoscope: a travel company discovered Burraka, built a landing strip and a city of holiday chalets, and was flying in hordes of tourists. Then a warlord called Tom Toby, Oxford-educated, English-speaking, and savage under the thinnest of veneers, marched in with his ragtag army. He deposed the ruler of Burraka, and probably ate him, occupied the palace, confiscated the holiday business, seized the land and gave it to his followers, sold the Burrakans into slavery in the Middle East, and wrecked that fertile valley with its temperate climate by diverting its water supply and demolishing a mountain ostensibly to make a road to the wealthy east and thus letting in alien air and weather.

Mary prayed for both Rudy and Zac: because of the rape of Burraka they had gone to fight for a better world in the Spanish Civil War. Her sons had been distressed to think of the fate of the sweet obliging girls they had swum with, and the children who were more than likely theirs. Perhaps in Spain they could make amends for their selfishness.

Instead, they were disillusioned, their distress was compounded by disillusion. They had meant to be stretcher-bearers, but rifles were thrust into their hands on arrival and they were ordered to spend three months in a trench in Northern Spain in winter. They were never in danger, and they and the other foreign volunteers had nothing much to do, except grind their political axes. However the war began, it had become a battle or a rehearsal of battle between Hitler and Stalin. Its achievements to date, so far as representatives of the Band of Hope could see, were a few massacres and forcing some nuns to jump off cliffs.

They walked away from it – not ran away, just walked across the border with Portugal and travelled back to Castle Scar like homing pigeons. The family was relieved – the relief was mutual. Zac resumed work on his study of social services, and Mary worried. Was Zac going to make everyone more or less poor and more or less ill? Was Rudy about to do field trials of the drugs that he believed would be the remedy for all that was wrong with the world? Was he going to endanger his health and destroy his mind by experimenting with poisonous pills?

Just as Mary's bad news about one of her children was often mitigated by good news in respect of another, so a little worry could be replaced by a big problem. Addie with her three babies was short of everything, energy, money, an extra pair of hands, and love. Mary was afraid that a woman without good looks in her late twenties with three little fatherless brown boys, and virtually no dowry, would not find a lover, let alone a husband. The irony of it made matters worse, for Addie was the self-appointed champion of love set free by foolproof contraception, and might never find a man to make love with her. The best contraceptive on the cards of the future was of no use to her whatsoever – what she wanted was a man now and on any terms.

What was to be done?

Mary had yet another child to comfort. Owing to the increasing likelihood of war, the high command of the armed forces had been putting heavy pressure on Viv's Cambridge team to hurry up and produce a viable atomic bomb. He kept on assuring his mother and the rest of the family that he had participated in research into atomic energy for peaceful purposes, not war; but his concern was obvious and could trigger another breakdown. When he promised everyone that an atomic bomb would be far too destructive ever to be dropped in anger, Mary, notwithstanding her fears that it might be the death of innumerable innocents, had to pretend to believe him.

She had a birthday round about this time, and five of her eight children attended the dinner party in her honour – Magda in Germany, Winnie in France were missing, and Noah was dead. Edward proposed the toast to her at the end of the meal.

He said: 'I'm not going to pay her the compliments she deserves, they'd embarrass her. So I'm just going to drink the health of my much better half and ask you all to join in.'

Then there were calls for her to reply: 'Speech, speech!'

Mary at length said, laughing: 'Edward, darling Edward, you've told them a fib, and it's the first fib I've heard you tell after all these years – I'm not better than you, never was and never could be. There! And you, my children, you're simply the best in my opinion. Thank you for being so good to me in spite of my follies and failings.'

Addie then spoke.

'Really, Mother, why do you insist on being such an impossibly hard act to follow?'

And Phil, too, had something to say: 'I'm not going to make a speech. We never have speeches at our birthday dinners. I don't know why we're having speeches tonight. I'm hoping it's not because there may be horrible things waiting to happen, war and danger, war and upheaval.'

Her brothers soothed her feelings, then Rudy said a few words.

'Well, Mother, I'll pay you a compliment, but

you can think it isn't complimentary if you like. My brothers and I are still bachelors because none of us can find females who are anything like you.'

EDWARD

Edward talked to his gardener, Jones, as he did not talk to his wife. He talked as men do to one another, and no doubt the same applies to women. Mary might have called Edward's talk to Jones cynical, but Jones understood that it was realistic, objective, practical.

Edward in 1938 had hair turning white and getting thin on top. His left leg that had been broken by shrapnel was gammy, and two fingers of his left hand had curled up owing to the wound that damaged the tendons. His breathing was sometimes laboured thanks to the gas he had inhaled in the war. But his health was not too bad – his health was surprisingly good considering he had been sure when the war ended that he only had a short time to live.

Jones in 1938 was strong almost as ever. Working on a Gloucestershire farm with his father from the age of twelve, followed by four years in the trenches, seemed to have done him no lasting harm; and his nearly twenty years of happy marriage, secure employment, and outdoor life on a Cornish cliff-top must have been salutary. His children, James and Iris, had grown up, at least they were the right age to do war work;

but neither Jones nor his wife Jean showed outward signs of being unduly worried by politics and the international news.

The association of Edward and Jones in 1914 set a sociological example. Edward had been well educated, Jones left school early. Edward became a stockbroker while Jones fed ailing lambs from a milk bottle in sheds in the Cotswolds on cold spring days and nights. Edward was the son of a lord who lived in a castle. But death, and the closeness to it, is a great leveller. Edward was not a snob, nor was Jones an inverted one: they were equally prepared to judge on evidence. They did their jobs to each other's satisfaction. Edward was cleverer than Jones in some ways, and vice versa – Jones was cleverer in country ways, judging the lie of land, shooting straight, And when the killing began, and blood flowed, they had held their nerves. Occasionally, after saving each other's lives or attending to a fallen comrade, they had exchanged glances communicative not exactly of gratitude or sentiment, but of acknowledgement that tests were being passed.

The armistice coincided with the death of Edward's parents, and his inheritance of the title and Castle Scar. He offered Jones the job of gardener, and the story of their peacetime association began.

The third Baron Penzoote, a civilian in his late thirties, husband, father, investor and gentleman, had been an only child, innately anti-social, and somehow detached. These charac-teristics were aggravated in the so-called Great

War. He suffered in his soul as well as physically. He never had many male friends, and he lost all of them in the fighting. He did not take his seat in the House of Lords – was disinclined to lay down the law; seldom went to London; was reclusive but tolerant of the hospitable impulses of his wife and children – he had taken very early retirement from the active life he was neither fit for nor disposed to lead. He mentally divided his post-war existence into three – publicly at ease and capable of jollity in moderation; in the privacy of his carefully constructed routine, content; and in secret battling against his first-hand observation of the vileness of mankind in general, and begging his god to help to dispel his melancholia.

His toast to Mary was no fib – she kept him from drowning in a sea of pessimism. She was his better half because he would have been so much worse without her. His children were a distraction that cut both ways. And then there was Jones – Jones was down to earth in every sense, straightforward and true, and their exchange of views on non-horticultural subjects was a safety-valve. Moreover, while respecting the etiquette of rank, military and otherwise, they proved that hierarchy is no bar to friendship.

Edward attended to financial business on weekday mornings. He read newspapers and spoke to his stockbroker. He was feeding his family by playing the market cautiously: he did not often do deals, but managed to make enough money to pay the bills and not to lose it too often. In the afternoons he pottered in the garden, was available for tea parties and family obligations. In the evenings in summer he would air his opinions of the opinions his children had aired at dinner, chatting with Jones over the picket fence. When night fell early in winter, beside a bonfire of Jones's making or, if it rained, in the kitchen of Garden Cottage, he would discuss his children and set the world to rights.

He said on different occasions: 'My children are nice people, and I love them, I enjoy them, but I've come to the conclusion they're mistaken. Remember Magda, she fell for a man who's now the Demon King of the universal panto. Remember Noah, he died in Stalin's trousers – what a farce, what a waste! And Winnie and Addie were caught napping by babies. And Rudy wants to shut out the world by means of drugs, and Zac would force you and me to pay other people's doctors' bills, and Viv's working overtime on a bomb that'll blow us all to smithereens. Phil's a bit dotty, but at least she can see that it might be a better idea to stand still than to behave like lemmings – lemmings regularly commit communal suicide...

'The Band of Hope thinks it's philanthropic. But everyone's still hoping, the Band of Hope hasn't done any good so far, and I can't help wondering what will become of all of us in the future, supposing the philanthropy of my children is forced down our throats. Hitler was Magda's heart's desire and inspiration, and wants war, he's a warmonger, he'll drag us into the worst war

206

ever fought – if he conquers us we'll be crushed and squashed, and if we conquer him we'll be impoverished and won't recover for ages, perhaps ever. Winnie would have the laws of love amended so that any poorer person could claim half the fortune of any richer person he or she has slept with, lived with or married. Winnie would like to help women, but thieves would be mainly helped by her bright idea, helped to help themselves. Noah gave his life for a phoney religion that's begun to wreck this century and is bound to create more mayhem before people see through it. Rudy's a casualty of Africa, one of the many, and he believes in drugs. He thinks we'd be and do better if we were turned chemically into other people. He's a lazy fellow, always was, and never read any of the books written by the victims of their addiction to substances that robbed them of their lives. Poor Addie! She was such a law-abiding citizen, she only broke one law, and now she's for closing the stable door after the horse has bolted. Think of the side-effects of the contraceptive pill she's pining for: promiscuity without fears or tears, jealousy given grounds to be more jealous, giddy young girls forgetting to take their medicine, more abortions, more hearts and homes broken, more of the children of divorces damaged beyond repair, and more of their parents paying exorbitant fees to break their promises and be rid of partners! Oh well! Oh hell! Zac to the rescue with his politicians acting as doctors! Zac's health service would be one of the biggest businesses in the world, how on earth could politicians run it? Modern politicians are only there because of the gift of the gab, they only know how to spend money, tax us and spend it – a few exceptions prove that rule. Doctors and hospitals paid for by the government – consequences, the country on its uppers, monolithic muddles, and complaints all round. Perhaps Viv's bomb will do us a favour. If he can make a bomb, so can other scientists in other countries, and sooner or later one will come our way and give the survivors a chance to start again from scatch and maybe build a land fit for decent folk to live in...

'I love my children. Seriously, I'm proud of them. They can't be called ordinary. They're idealists, not money-grubbers: which, I'm sorry to say, is a pity – they never count the cost of their ideals. They're intellectuals, you see, and liberals. They think, they think of what would be good for us, and they think they're right, ignoring nature, leaving nature out of all their calculations, human nature and the rules of the natural kingdom that we break at our peril...

'I bless my children for one reason in particular: they've never turned completely against their religion. As a rule, liberal intellectuals can't stand anyone who's above them, or more bossy than they are. They can't approve of a god who is not only more equal than others but almighty. And they're sure they know more than ritualistic priests and superstitious worshippers of a will of the wisp. My children have never stopped thinking that God is God, and sometimes

I've wondered what God might think of them. How popular are my children in the House of the Lord, the residence of the All-powerful, or unpopular? Great lords in the olden times employed jesters to cheer them up and make them laugh. King Lear had a fool, and the ruler of the Kingdom in his power and glory could have eight fools. The plots and plans of the Band of Hope would no doubt bring a wry smile to the features of our Lord, and his compassion would have mercy on their presumptuous prophecies. I quite like to look upon my children as the fools of God.'

Edward Penzoote spread these assessments over many months of chatting with Jones. He listened as well as speaking, answered Jones's questions about investment, and gave advice in return for advice. And another winter went by, and the spring of 1939 showed it was on the way in the English manner, by means of frosts and gales.

One rainy afternoon while the two old friends sheltered in the potting shed, Edward said: 'The Band of Hope seems more hopeless with every day that passes. Politicians got us into one war and now seem to be getting us into another. My children have always denied they're politicians, they say they're sociologists or something; but I've a nasty feeling that after this war we'll have all my children's pet schemes imposed upon us, egalitarianism, populism, drugs, sex and longevity courtesy of Dr Government. And will we live to see nature having its revenge on the arrogant provocations of the new social order? There'll be a lot of hypocrisy and corruption before the atom bomb sends everybody packing.'

On another afternoon he said: 'I mustn't grumble. Lady Luck's smiled at me, and I'm more than grateful. I believe you'd say the same, Jones, if I ever gave you a chance to speak. Wars are usually declared in the autumn. Here's hoping we have a warm summer, then we'll have to grit our teeth and wait to see what the younger generation will be prepared to do to us and for us.'

'Yes, sir,' Jones replied.

'Sorry I've bent your ear for all our years together, Jones.'

'It's been interesting, sir.'

'There was something else I wanted to tell you, but what was it? I've forgotten. It doesn't matter.'

'Weather's clearing up. If you'll pardon me, sir, I've work to get on with.'

'You've said it, Jones.'